CRUEL COMMENTS

Veronica brought her horse, Danny, to a square halt. She looked down at Emily with an expression of smug satisfaction. "You know, this is what *real* riding is all about."

Stevie moved closer to Emily. "Let's go," she whispered. "She isn't going to change."

Veronica either didn't hear or pretended not to. "You might want to come watch us compete next weekend," she continued. "It'll all be real riding—a lot different from those pony rides they take you on at Free Rein."

Emily flushed red. "I ride," she said.

Veronica smiled. "I'm sure you do," she said. "You should try to come next weekend. Then maybe you'd understand."

"Come on," Stevie whispered fiercely, her hand on Emily's elbow. "Don't listen to anything she says."

Emily nodded and turned back to the stable, but The Saddle Club could see that their friend's eyes were full of tears.

THE SADDLE CLUB

RIDING CLASS

BONNIE BRYANT

A SKYLARK BOOK

NEW YORK • TORONTO • LONDON • SYDNEY • AUCKLAND

RL 5, 009–012

RIDING CLASS
A Skylark Book / March 1996

ISBN 0-553-48362-5

Published simultaneously in the United States and Canada

Bantam Books are published by Bantam Books, a division of Bantam Doubleday Dell Publishing Group, Inc. Its trademark, consisting of the words
"Bantam Books" and the portrayal of a rooster, is Registered in U.S. Patent
and Trademark Office and in other countries. Marca Registrada. Bantam
Books, 1540 Broadway, New York, New York 10036.

PRINTED IN THE UNITED STATES OF AMERICA
OPM   0 9 8 7 6 5 4 3 2

*I would like to express my special thanks to
Kimberly Brubaker Bradley
for her help in the writing of this book.*

*I would also like to give my sincere thanks to a number of
people who helped with ideas, information, and most of all
inspiration for this story: Joyce Mabry and the Therapeutic
Riding Association of Virginia; Patty Pryor at A Leg
Up Riding Center in Abingdon, Virginia; the North
American Riding for the Handicapped Association; and
the Agape Therapeutic Riding Center of Cicero, Indiana.*

1

"HORSE WISE, COME to order!"

With a last-second flurry of whispers, the members of Horse Wise, the Pony Club at Pine Hollow Stables, hurried to find seats on the office floor. Stevie Lake dashed in late and looked around the room for her two best friends, Lisa Atwood and Carole Hanson. Lisa waved Stevie over to the seat she and Carole had saved.

"Thanks! I knew I could count on you!" Stevie said. "Won't this be fun? I wish we were riding, but still—"

"Horse Wise, come to *order*," Max Regnery said again, with an amused glance in Stevie's direction. Stevie grinned but quit talking. Max ran Horse Wise in addition to own-

1

ing and running Pine Hollow Stables. Max was the boss, and he hated it when his students didn't listen to what he had to say. Fortunately for the students, what Max had to say was usually very worthwhile. It was usually about horses.

Stevie, Lisa, and Carole were united by a common love of horses and riding. They'd met and become best friends at Pine Hollow, and they spent most of their free time there. The three girls had even formed The Saddle Club, which was devoted to learning more about riding. There were only two rules: Members had to be horse-crazy, and they had to be willing to help each other out.

Of the three, Carole was considered the best rider. She was crazy about horses and planned to spend her life working with them—whether as a rider, trainer, or vet, she wasn't quite sure. Stevie had no idea what she wanted to do when she grew up—she was having too much fun right now to worry about her future. Stevie's love of practical jokes sometimes landed her in serious trouble, but her creative solutions—and her two best friends—usually got her out. Lisa was older, and more serious, than the other two. She hadn't been riding for as long, but she was working hard to catch up.

"First things first," Max continued, and the three girls, along with the other twenty or so members of Horse Wise, sat up straight and listened. "Thank you all for being so willing to give up your mounted meeting today. We'll also have an unmounted meeting next weekend, but after that . . . well, I'll make it up to you."

As with most Pony Clubs, Horse Wise usually alternated between mounted—on horseback—and unmounted—classroom—meetings. Today they would have had a mounted meeting, but instead they were joining several other nearby Pony Clubs, hunt clubs, and riding clubs to work on Volunteer Day at Free Rein, a local center for therapeutic riding.

"There will definitely be a mounted meeting two weeks from now," Max went on. "Let's just say that those of you who haven't been riding much this winter might want to make an effort to get back in the saddle before then. Let's just say," he paused, looking around the room at the rapt faces of his riders, "that there might be prizes involved." He grinned. *Like a cat in the cream*, Carole thought. It was a typical Max expression.

"Prizes!" squealed May Grover, one of the younger riders. "He means a horse show!"

The Saddle Club smiled. Winter was over, but barely. The horses still wore their thick winter coats, and the riders usually did, too. The paddocks were muddy from melted snow and cold winter rain, and the horses were often muddy from rolling in the paddocks. Stevie, Carole, and Lisa were more dedicated than most of the other riders at Pine Hollow, but when the indoor arena was being used for lessons, and the trails and outdoor ring were hock-deep in slick, half-frozen mud, even The Saddle Club couldn't possibly ride. They were eager for spring. A horse show would be a fantastic change of pace.

"Well," said a snooty voice from the back, "we know who'll win the championship, don't we?"

The Saddle Club didn't have to look to know who *that* was. Veronica diAngelo, their least favorite rider of all time, had gotten a new horse named Danny for Christmas. At least, Danny was what people called him. His registered name—his show name—was Go For Blue. Stevie also had her own horse, a mare named Belle, and Carole had a bay gelding named Starlight. They were both fantastic horses, but their show names were Belle and Starlight, and even Stevie and Carole had to admit that in terms of equine perfection, they didn't come close to Danny. He was like a Greek god: aloof, impeccable, flawless. And Veronica, who'd always attached tremendous importance to money and prestige, was a real brat about him.

Lisa leaned over to whisper to her friends. "The worst part is, she's probably right." Carole nodded grimly, and Stevie made a face. On her bad days, Veronica had temper tantrums, but on her good days she rode very well indeed. She and Danny would certainly go for blue—for the blue ribbon that would be first prize.

"Oh, I wouldn't be so sure about that," Max said, startling The Saddle Club, who weren't sure if he was talking to them or responding to Veronica's comment. "This—er —event may be a little—umm—different." He paused, then shook his head, still smiling. "I'll tell you all the details next week. Meanwhile, I hereby challenge all of you who've been stuck in the winter doldrums to shake the wind out of your sails, turn over a new leaf, put your noses to the grindstone, and—" Max seemed to get lost in his metaphors—"and anyway, let's have a quick review before we head off to Free Rein. Who read the pamphlets I sent home with you last week?"

Every hand went up. Max seemed pleased. "Very good. Then tell me, when did therapeutic riding begin in this country?"

Meg Durham answered. "In the late 1960s. It started in Europe before that."

"Right. And what is therapeutic riding?"

Adam raised his hand. "Riding done by people with physical, mental, or emotional disabilities. It helps them become stronger, like physical therapy. And it helps them learn new skills."

5

"And it's fun," Carole added. "They get to ride horses." To her, that was the most important part. Carole couldn't imagine her life without horses, and she knew how much they had helped her emotional state in the terrible months just before and after her mother's death.

"Right," Max said. "Now, today at Free Rein we aren't going to see any riding, and we may not see much of the horses. But just remember why we're doing this: so someone else gets to ride." He clapped his hands together. "Let's go! We've got work to do!"

Laughing and talking, Horse Wise piled out of the office and into the cars that were waiting to take them to Free Rein. The Saddle Club headed for Carole's father's station wagon. Colonel Hanson was a Horse Wise volunteer.

"We can take a few more people!" Carole called. Meg and Polly Giacomin came running. "Veronica?" As soon as she said that, Carole wished she hadn't. Even if Free Rein was only a few miles away, the last thing Carole wanted to do was spend those miles in the same car with Veronica. But Veronica was heading—alone—to her family's chauffeur-driven Mercedes.

Veronica stopped and turned. "My family supports the poor by generous financial contributions," she informed Carole. "We don't feel the need to get *involved* with them."

"Of course," Carole responded numbly, stopping in her

6

tracks. Veronica smiled and climbed into the Mercedes. The chauffeur closed the door for her.

"Of course," Carole repeated, getting into the station wagon with a shake of her head. "She's Veronica." Colonel Hanson pulled out of the drive.

"She isn't coming to Free Rein, is she?" Lisa asked.

"She called them 'the poor,' " Carole said, still amazed.

"They can't be poor. They're riders," Stevie said.

"I thought Max said no one at Free Rein had to pay for lessons," Meg said.

"It's a United Way–sponsored agency," Colonel Hanson explained. "People pay what they can."

"Veronica's a nincompoop," Stevie said. "Remember what a snot she was about the benefit we did for the County Animal Rescue League? She never puts herself out for anyone."

"She doesn't understand anything about helping anyone," Lisa said. She was grateful for the support her friends gave her and glad when she could help them back. It was a feeling Veronica didn't understand, and Lisa almost felt sorry for her. Almost.

"It doesn't matter," Colonel Hanson said. "You'll have a better day without her. Here we are!" He pulled into a freshly paved parking lot. Right in front of them was a large, tan indoor arena. Behind that nestled a smaller tan building that looked like a stable, and on both sides were

7

big paddocks containing a variety of fuzzy, sturdy, placid-looking horses. A paper banner on the side of the arena read, WELCOME, VOLUNTEERS!

"Isn't this fun?" Lisa asked as they got out of the car. Stevie and Carole nodded. The parking lot was packed, and there were people everywhere.

"I just wish Cross County had come," Stevie said with a dramatic sigh. Carole and Lisa laughed. Stevie's boyfriend, Phil, rode with Cross County Pony Club.

"Look at it this way, you'll get more work done without him," Carole teased. She led the way into a door on the side of the arena.

The door led to a lounge with wide windows looking into the arena. A big couch, a table, and several comfortable chairs were scattered around. On the couch a tiger cat lay contentedly, nursing three tiny kittens. The room was full of people of all ages.

"Welcome," said a deep, friendly voice. A red-haired woman near the table stood up and waved her arms to attract attention. "I'm Debbie Payne, director of Free Rein Therapeutic Riding Center. I'm delighted that so many of you have given up your Saturday to come here. We always get a lot of work done on Volunteer Day. Your help is invaluable.

"We don't have any lessons going on today," she continued. "But all of you are welcome to come back another

8

day. We now have twelve horses, some two hundred regular volunteers, and just over one hundred riders.

"I'll be around all day, and if any of you have questions about Free Rein, please ask. Meanwhile, there are doughnuts, coffee, and juice on the side of the room. We'll set out a lunch at noon. Now, let's get to work! Who here has carpentry experience?"

"OUCH!" LISA CRIED an hour later. She dropped her hammer and sucked her thumb, then examined it closely. The Saddle Club was standing in Free Rein's west paddock. "I can't believe you told her we had carpentry experience," she said to Stevie.

"I didn't actually say 'carpentry experience,' " Stevie replied. "I said, 'I think we can hammer nails.' "

"Maybe *you* can hammer," Lisa said. "I can't."

"Did you hurt yourself?" Stevie bent over her friend's hand. "Are you okay?" The three girls had been replacing broken and horse-chewed rails in the paddock fence.

"Suck it," Carole advised.

"I did."

"You hold the boards," Stevie suggested. "Let me do the nailing."

"Okay." They worked without talking for a while.

"One thing," Lisa finally said, "it's nice to be outside on a sunny day like this. It even smells like spring."

9

"And we're near some horses, even though they're ignoring us," said Carole. Three horses were grazing in the paddock where The Saddle Club was working.

"I thought this sounded like a better job than fixing the kick boards in the arena," said Stevie.

"Or painting ground poles," Lisa agreed.

"Or cleaning out the tack room," said Carole. "We do enough of that at Pine Hollow. I wish they had wanted us to groom or do something that actually involved the horses, but, like Max said, we're doing this so someone else can ride."

"Not really ride," objected Stevie. She concentrated fiercely, took aim, and squarely hit the nail she was holding. Lisa flinched. "Ha! Got it!" Stevie cried. "I don't think a strong, tight paddock fence helps anyone ride," she added. "I think it helps keep the horses safe so people can ride them."

Carole laughed. "Picky, picky," she said.

"Having fun, girls?" They turned. Ms. Payne had walked across the paddock to meet them. "You're doing a great job," she said. She reached into her pocket and pulled out a Band-Aid, which she handed to Lisa with a wink.

"Thanks. We're trying," Lisa said. Stevie and Carole snorted. They introduced themselves.

"From Pine Hollow!" Ms. Payne exclaimed. "That

chestnut horse in the center paddock, over there, he came from Pine Hollow, too. His name is Jeremiah."

Stevie frowned. "I don't remember him," she said, "and I've been riding at Pine Hollow for a long time."

"Jerry's been here almost ten years," Ms. Payne replied. "He's one of our steadiest and best horses, as well as one of our oldest. Sometimes our horses get a little bored here—it's slow work for them, they don't get to canter much, and they never jump—so whenever they start to seem bored we loan them to a regular lesson program for a little while, and bring them back after they've had a vacation. Jeremiah never needs one."

"Did you buy him from Max?" Carole asked.

Ms. Payne shook her head, smiling. "No, actually, Max gave him to us," she said. "Jeremiah was getting old, and his arthritis made it uncomfortable for him to work hard. But he's the type of horse that loves people and wants to be used. Our program's a perfect way for him to spend his retirement, precisely because it is such slow work. He's over thirty years old."

"Wow!" Carole knew that horses rarely lived that long. "Are all of your horses so old?"

"Thankfully, no, but most are at least middle-aged. The youngest is eleven. Horses used for therapeutic riding have to be exceptionally calm and quiet so that they never do anything that might hurt the riders. It takes time for a horse to mellow out. Most young ones are still too excitable."

Stevie understood. If something startled Belle, the mare could jump sideways like a cat. "I don't think my horse would do well here," she told Ms. Payne. "Not now, and maybe not ever."

"Not Starlight, either," Carole agreed. "He's good and well behaved, but he pays attention to everything, and sometimes he gets a little distracted."

Lisa laughed. "And definitely not Prancer!" she said, referring to the Pine Hollow horse she usually rode. "Prancer's a Thoroughbred," she explained. "She used to be a racehorse, so she's pretty high-strung."

Ms. Payne laughed, too. "You're probably right," she said. "All of you, in fact. You won't find any Thoroughbreds here. As a breed, they're generally considered too 'hot' for our needs. Arabs too. We like mixed-breed horses, especially horses with some kind of draft breed in them— what you'd call cold-blooded horses.

"Even then," she continued, "we look for an exceptional temperament."

Ms. Payne looked around the paddocks with satisfaction. "These horses may not look like much, but they're very special animals. To us, they're worth their weight in gold.

12

Thanks for helping, girls. If you need anything, just yell, and don't forget to go in and take a break when you need one." The Saddle Club thanked her, and Ms. Payne walked over to the next group of volunteers.

"Ha!" Stevie said, resuming her pounding with vigor. "At last we've discovered something that Veronica's horse can't do! He wouldn't be a good therapeutic horse!"

"Don't bet on it," Carole said gloomily.

"I don't mind getting my fingers smashed," Lisa cut in, "but I hate to spoil this beautiful day by talking about Veronica."

"Here, here," Stevie agreed. "Sometimes silence is golden."

WHEN THEY RAN out of nails, The Saddle Club walked toward the back of the stable to get more. The stable was bigger than it looked from the front. Probably, Carole thought, casting an eye over it, there was room for sixteen horses, maybe more. Free Rein still had room to expand.

"The door's open," she said. "It wasn't before."

Stevie grinned. "Let's look."

"I'm not sure we're supposed to go in there," Lisa objected.

"Why not?" Stevie asked. "They must need help in the

barn, too. We could muck stalls or something. Listen! Someone's already working."

"Back it up," The Saddle Club heard an authoritative voice say from the stable aisle. "Now whoa, stand still. That's it. Good boy."

"Someone's talking to a horse," Carole said. Her eyes gleamed.

"Where did you find all this mud?" the voice continued. "P.C., it's going to take me forever to get you clean!" The voice sounded like a girl—a girl about the age of The Saddle Club. They walked through the stable door. At the other end of the aisle a stocky palomino stood on cross-ties. On the far side of the horse stood a slight girl with brunet hair.

"Hi!" Carole said, walking toward her, with Stevie and Lisa close behind. "Can we help?"

The girl looked up and smiled. "I'm fine," she said.

"We were hoping to do something with the horses," Lisa explained. "How did you get the job?" She moved toward the side of the horse and stopped. The girl wore metal braces on both her legs. She leaned heavily on one cuffed crutch and groomed the palomino awkwardly with her other hand.

"P.C.'s my horse," the girl said. She turned to look at them, and as she did, the tip of her crutch slipped on the

14

concrete floor. She crashed to the ground. Her crutch hit the horse hard on the knees, and she rolled right between his forelegs.

The Saddle Club gasped. If the horse moved, the girl would be trampled!

CAROLE KNEW JUST what to do. Walking quickly but calmly, she moved to the horse's head and held it still. "Lisa, Stevie," she directed, "help her!" Stevie reached for the girl, but the girl shook her head.

"Please don't hold my horse," she said, politely but firmly. "He's fine. You don't need to help me. Just give me room."

Carole dropped her hands from the horse's halter, feeling embarrassed. Hadn't she done the right thing? She knew not to spook the horse, and it certainly looked as if the girl needed help. The girl was struggling to get her weight underneath her and the cuff of the crutch around her left arm. Meanwhile her horse stood like a stone statue. He hadn't moved, Carole realized, not even when the girl had fallen. "Good boy," Carole said softly to him.

Stevie had been ready to rush in and lift the girl back to her feet. It was a Saddle Club rule: Help whenever help was needed. Not just when help was wanted, but when it was needed. Maybe the girl didn't want their help, but did she need it? Stevie felt her fingers itch with impatience. She forced herself to stand still.

When Stevie had overheard the girl talking to her horse, she had thought the girl was another rider, like The Saddle Club. But now, staring at the girl's leg braces and crutches and the slow, tense way she moved, Stevie thought that the girl wasn't actually anything like them at all.

Then she realized that she had thought wrong. Take away the leg braces and the girl looked just like them. She was dressed the same, in a sweater, jeans, and paddock boots. Her shiny brown hair was pulled into a ponytail. And obviously she loved horses.

The girl used one of the horse's sturdy legs to pull herself to her feet. She leaned against him unsteadily and gave him a pat. "Way to go, buddy," she told him. "Another gold star for you." She turned to The Saddle Club and smiled. "I'm Emily. Emily Williams."

17

"I'm Lisa Atwood," Lisa said. She introduced the rest of The Saddle Club. "We're with Horse Wise Pony Club, and we're here for Volunteer Day." Lisa felt a little awkward, but she knew her manners. Her mother had once told her that good manners could carry a person through any social situation.

Emily laughed. "Volunteer Day is the reason I can't ride today," she said. "But it'll be great to have the arena back in good shape. Is Pony Club fun? I always thought it would be."

"It's terrific fun," Lisa answered. "Are you sure you're okay? That looked like a pretty hard fall."

"I'll have a few bruises." Emily shrugged. "I usually do. I'm used to it. Thanks for not helping."

"That doesn't make sense," Stevie said, her feeling of awkwardness vanishing. "Why should you thank us for not doing anything?"

"Because you didn't! And that's just what I wanted you to do!" Emily said. Her eyebrows went up and she grinned at Stevie.

Stevie grinned back. "That sounds like something I would say when I want to confuse my little brother," Stevie said.

"Does it confuse *you*?" Emily asked. Her face took on a mischievous look. "I'm not talking too fast for you, am I?

18

My mom always says I talk too fast. Am-I-talking-too-fast?" She sped through the last words.

"Not-at-all," said Stevie, just as quickly.

"AmItalkingtoofastforyounow?"

"*AlmostbutnotquiteIthinkIcantalkfasterthanyou.*"

"That's enough!" Lisa said, as Stevie and Emily dissolved into giggles. "Is it true what you said? Do people really insist on doing things for you?"

Emily rolled her eyes. "All the time," she said. "It's unbelievable. I mean, sometimes I do need help, but when I do, I ask for it. Old women on the street say, 'Oh, you poor dear.'" Her voice rose high, mimicking.

Carole was still patting the palomino. "This is a super horse," she declared. "He's amazing."

Emily looked at him fondly. "He's the best horse ever."

"How long have you had him?" Lisa asked. She wished that she had a horse of her own.

"I got him for Christmas last year," Emily replied. "I sort of knew I was going to get him, because we had to look so long to find him. But he was still the best present ever. His name's P.C." She bent over slowly, holding on to P.C.'s leg, to retrieve the rubber currycomb she'd dropped when she'd fallen. The rest of her grooming gear sat on a waist-high shelf on the side of the aisle. She began to curry P.C.

19

"Can't we help?" Carole asked. "We'd like to . . . it's been four hours since we touched a horse!"

"Sure," said Emily. She handed them brushes and they got to work on P.C. He had rolled hard, and his coat was thick with dried mud. Dust flew as the girls worked the dirt loose.

"What's P.C. stand for?" asked Stevie. She sneezed.

"Personal Computer. Just kidding," Emily added quickly. "It stands for Palomino Cow pony."

"Oh, wow, do you ride Western?" Stevie exclaimed. "I know a great pinto cow pony out West. His name is Stewball, and he's a cutting horse at a ranch our friend Kate owns—I mean her family owns the ranch—and he's a fantastic horse, too. I almost bought him once, but it turned out he was happier on the ranch. My horse, Belle, is better for the kind of riding I like best."

Lisa and Carole laughed. Usually Carole was the one who got carried away when talking about horses.

"I ride English, not Western," Emily said. "I think jumping looks fun, but they don't teach it at Free Rein, so I've never tried it. What I really like is dressage."

Stevie's jaw dropped. "Me too. That's my absolute favorite kind of riding."

"Neat," said Emily. "Most people don't even know what 'dressage' means."

"The word 'dressage' just means training," Carole said.

20

"I like dressage, too, but Starlight, my horse, is better at jumping."

Carole had ridden simple dressage tests with Starlight before. The tests were precise patterns ridden one at a time in a flat arena. It often amused Lisa and Carole that Stevie, who was boisterous and somewhat disorganized, was so good at a controlled, highly organized sport like dressage. Belle was becoming good, too.

"What does your horse like?" Emily asked, turning to Lisa.

"Prancer doesn't know yet," Lisa said. "She isn't my horse, either, but she's the one I usually ride." Lisa described the Pine Hollow lesson horse to Emily.

Emily bent over slowly, and carefully tugged at P.C.'s leg. P.C. lifted his foot immediately, and Emily cleaned the mud out of his hoof with a pick. "I guess P.C. doesn't know what he likes best, either," she said, her voice somewhat muffled from leaning against P.C.'s flank. "He does everything I ask, but he doesn't exactly look like a dressage horse, does he? His neck is three feet wide."

"He looks like a great horse," Carole said, although she could see that P.C. did have a very thick neck.

"He's perfect and he's beautiful and he's tremendously ugly," Emily said, straightening up and beginning to slowly make her way down P.C.'s side. "Facts are facts."

"There you go not making sense again," Stevie said.

21

"You thanked us for what we didn't do, and now you say your ugly horse is beautiful. Or your beautiful horse is ugly." Stevie grimaced; she hadn't meant to call P.C. ugly. Most of the lesson horses at Pine Hollow wouldn't win any beauty contests either, but they were good horses and Stevie loved them all.

"Whichever," Emily said agreeably. "Facts are facts." She lifted and cleaned P.C.'s rear hoof, then held on to his tail for balance while she moved behind him to his other side.

Carole began to brush P.C.'s mane. It was soft and nearly tangle-free, which Carole knew meant that Emily probably combed it out almost every day. "You must spend a lot of time here," she said to Emily.

"I do," Emily replied. "I love it. I can't remember when I didn't love horses. I've been riding since I was four years old."

"You started even earlier than I did," Carole said.

"You started earlier than any of us," Lisa added.

Emily finished picking out P.C.'s hooves, then collected the grooming tools from them and put them in her bucket. "I started as soon as the center opened," she said. "My pediatrician rides, and she knew it would be good for me, so she signed me up right away.

"I have cerebral palsy," she continued. "That means my

brain was injured somehow before I was born. Cerebral palsy affects people different ways, but in my case it means my muscles, especially in my legs, don't work right. They're too tight, sort of. I can't move my legs easily, and I don't have very good balance. That's why I fall down."

"Does it get worse?" Lisa asked. She wasn't sure if it was a polite question, but she wanted to know.

"No," Emily said. "Muscular dystrophy can get worse, but C.P.—cerebral palsy—doesn't. I'm a lot more mobile now than I used to be. Riding has really helped me a lot."

" 'P.C.' is the opposite of 'C.P.'," Carole realized.

"Yeah, but that's not why I call him that. I call him P.C. because he's my Prince Charming." Emily gave P.C. a hug.

"So is that why they call it therapeutic riding?" asked Stevie. "Because riding is your therapy?"

"Sure," said Emily. "It makes me stronger the same way that it makes you stronger. Only maybe it's better for me, because—well, you could ride a bike, right? And that would make you stronger, too. I can't ride a bike or—what else do you do? I can't do aerobics—"

"I suppose I could, but I wouldn't want to," Stevie cut in. "All that jumpy-dancey and spandex—ugh!"

Emily laughed but continued her explanation. "I do regular physical therapy—I call that P.T.—at home every morning. It helps me, but it's boring. Riding's different. It's . . . I don't know . . ."

"It's riding," Carole said.

"Exactly."

Lisa and Stevie nodded. They all understood.

Emily picked up a second crutch that had been leaning against the grooming shelf and fitted it to her arm. She pulled a blue lead rope off the shelf and snapped it to P.C.'s halter. Then she unfastened the two cross-tie snaps, which took her even longer. The Saddle Club didn't move.

"Thanks," Emily said softly, looking up at them. "I really do like to do things myself."

She began to lead P.C. down the aisle. As Emily walked, she swung her left crutch tip forward at the same time as her right leg. Then she paused and moved her right crutch forward along with her left leg. It was slow and halting, but P.C. matched her speed, keeping his nose exactly at Emily's shoulder. The Saddle Club watched them in admiration.

"You know," Lisa said, "we'd really like to learn more about therapeutic riding. Helping out today has been fun, but you're the only rider we've met, and we haven't gotten to see anyone ride. We like to learn everything about horses."

Emily put P.C. into his stall and slid the door closed. "If

you want to learn, you can," she said. "Free Rein always needs more volunteers to help with the riding lessons."

"Emily!" called a voice outside the stable.

"In here, Mom!" Emily called back.

A woman's head poked around the edge of the door. "Finished?" she asked. "We need to hurry—your brother's got a soccer game."

"Okay." Emily hung P.C.'s lead rope outside his stall. "It was fun talking to you," she said to The Saddle Club.

"Maybe we'll see you later," Stevie offered.

"That'd be nice." Emily smiled, but she looked a little doubtful. She waved to The Saddle Club and left with her mother.

"I mean it," Lisa said to Carole and Stevie. "I would like to learn more about therapeutic riding. I'd like to volunteer. Do you think we could make it a Saddle Club project?"

"I'd like to," Carole said.

"Me too," agreed Stevie.

They went in search of Ms. Payne. The director beamed when she heard that they wanted to volunteer. "We always need leaders and side-walkers," she said, "and the fact that you three already know how to take care of horses will be a big plus. When would you like to come?"

"How about Monday?" Stevie suggested. "After school?"

"That would be super. We've got a group lesson at four-thirty that isn't very advanced, so we need a lot of volunteers for that one," Ms. Payne said.

"Thank you," said Carole. She was pleased at the thought of learning something new.

"No, thank *you*," Ms. Payne corrected her. "Programs like Free Rein couldn't exist without volunteers."

ON SUNDAY AFTERNOON The Saddle Club met at Pine Hollow. It was a bright, sunny day, warm for early spring, and they decided to act on Max's advice—"Shake the wind out of our sails, whatever that means," Stevie said—and go on a trail ride. While they were gathering their tack and grooming buckets from the tack room, a thin, frail-looking, gray-haired woman wandered in.

"I wonder if you girls would know where I could find"—the woman consulted a scrap of paper—"a Mrs. Regnery? I'm supposed to have a lesson with her."

The girls exchanged glances. Max's wife, Deborah, was a Mrs. Regnery, but she was just learning to ride herself.

Max's mother, called Mrs. Reg for short, was also a Mrs. Regnery. She rode well but rarely gave lessons.

Lisa looked closely at the old woman and decided that Mrs. Reg must have offered to teach her so that the woman wouldn't be embarrassed about learning from someone young. The woman didn't look like a rider. She looked as if a puff of wind would knock her over. She wasn't dressed right, either. She had on crisp, new jeans; a fancy embroidered white blouse; and a very old pair of cowboy boots. Stevie often rode in jeans and cowboy boots, but on this woman they didn't look authentic: The jeans were too clean. Still, Lisa was impressed by the woman's bravery. It couldn't be easy for a person that old to start riding.

"Mrs. Reg's gone up to her house for a moment," Carole said. "She told us she'd be right back. Can we help you get started?" The sympathetic tone in Carole's voice told Lisa that her friend had drawn the same conclusions.

"Are you new here?" Stevie inquired solicitously. She'd never seen this woman at Pine Hollow before.

"I'm Dr. Marian Dinmore," the woman replied. "I live in Arizona, but I'm conducting a symposium at Georgetown medical school in Washington for the next several weeks, and I thought I'd take advantage of being on the East Coast. I always wanted to learn English riding."

"Did someone in Washington tell you about Pine Hollow?" Lisa asked. The capital wasn't far away, and they

28

often had members of Congress and other government officials at the stables. Once Lisa had taken a trail ride with an ambassador.

"No, I picked it out of the phone book," Dr. Dinmore replied. "Tell me, did I pick well?"

"Don't worry," Carole reassured her, "you picked very well. Pine Hollow is an excellent barn, the horses are very safe, and Mrs. Reg is a very nice person."

"They're very big on safety here," Lisa said. She took Dr. Dinmore's arm gently and guided her over to the good-luck horseshoe mounted on the wall. "You should touch this," she said, "it's one of our traditions. Everyone touches it before they ride, and no one has ever been seriously injured riding here."

"Not that you're going to be injured," Stevie said hastily. She couldn't believe Lisa, giving this poor woman a reason to be nervous! "The horses are terrific. They won't do anything to make you fall off, so you don't have to worry about that. But you should wear a riding helmet, just in case—" She pulled Dr. Dinmore into the locker room, where a pegboard covered with helmets took up a whole wall.

"I left my hat at home," Dr. Dinmore said. "It took up too much room in my suitcase."

"You need a special hat for riding," Stevie said. "It's not like a cowboy hat; it's more like a bike helmet. It's lightweight, but it's very protective." She pulled one of the helmets down and put it on Dr. Dinmore's head. The brim covered the woman's eyes. "Whoops—too big!"

Lisa handed Stevie a smaller hard hat. This one fit, and Carole reached out and buckled it beneath Dr. Dinmore's chin. "How does that feel?" Carole asked.

"Fine." Dr. Dinmore looked slightly amused. *She's probably not used to having people make this much of a fuss over her,* Carole thought. She was proud of herself and of The Saddle Club. They knew how to treat visitors at Pine Hollow. "Let's go find you a good horse," she suggested.

"Mrs. Reg's probably assigned her one already," Lisa said.

"Yes, but"—Carole shot Lisa a significant look—"we've met Dr. Dinmore, and we can probably do a better job finding her the right horse than Mrs. Reg. Mrs. Reg only talked to her on the phone."

Lisa understood. Mrs. Reg probably wouldn't have guessed how thin and frail and old Dr. Dinmore was. "That's right. We'll find you a horse that won't be too strong for you."

Dr. Dinmore laughed. "Girls, don't put me on an old plug!"

"Oh, no, we wouldn't do that," Carole said. "We don't have any bad horses at Pine Hollow. All of our horses will do what you tell them to do—at least, most of the time. But it's very important that you ride a quiet horse when you're just starting out." Carole patiently explained how a too-spirited horse could make learning to ride both difficult and scary.

Dr. Dinmore smiled gratefully. *She's glad that we're taking so much trouble over her*, Stevie decided. *She's glad that we really care*. "I think you might like Patch," she said.

"I completely agree," Carole said. "Patch is a wonderful horse." They led Dr. Dinmore to Patch's stall. Patch was an old pinto that many children took their first lessons on. His knees and feet were huge, like a draft horse's, and his head was thick and his neck was stubby. His eyes were kind.

"You won't have to worry about Patch running away with you," Lisa explained. "He can't go that fast."

Dr. Dinmore patted Patch's neck. "So this is the horse you all think suits me?"

Stevie nodded sincerely. "You'll be very safe with him," she said.

"Hello!" Mrs. Reg called down the aisle. "Are you Marian Dinmore?" She came up to them and shook Dr. Dinmore's hand.

"These girls have been showing me around," Dr. Dinmore said. "They've chosen a horse for me."

"Patch?" Mrs. Reg raised her eyebrows. "Why would— oh, never mind. Thank you for your help, girls. Go ahead and ride, now, and I'll help Dr. Dinmore."

As The Saddle Club returned to the tack room, they heard the two older women break into laughter. Lisa grinned. "It's not like Mrs. Reg to tell jokes," she said. "She must really be trying to put Dr. Dinmore at ease."

"I'm sure we helped, too," Carole said.

"Saddle Club projects all over the place," Stevie announced with satisfaction. "We've earned this trail ride!"

A HALF HOUR later, the girls were picking their way through a low spot in the corner of a field. "This is wet, but it's a lot drier than it was last week," Carole said. She gave Starlight his head and let him find the path he preferred.

"At least it's negotiable," Stevie agreed. She halted Belle and watched as Lisa coaxed Prancer through the puddle. "Poor Prancer! She doesn't like getting her feet wet," Stevie noted.

"Streams she likes, puddles she doesn't," Lisa said, laughing. "I don't understand Prancer sometimes."

"She's come a long way," Carole reminded her friend. "Trail riding isn't always easy—there are so many things that can distract the horses." As she spoke, Carole headed Starlight onto a trail through the woods. Ahead of them, an engine roared to life. Starlight wheeled around and bumped noses with Belle. Belle put her ears back and jumped sideways. Prancer jumped a little bit, too. "Whoa!" Carole said to Starlight. She turned him and urged him forward gently. Starlight shuddered, but took a step down the trail toward the noise.

The noise came around the corner and turned out to be a tractor. Max was driving it, pulling a load of hay bales on a trailer. He looked as startled to see The Saddle Club as the girls and their horses were to see him.

"Hello!" he said. He cut the engine and the horses quieted.

"What are you doing out here, Max?" Lisa asked.

"I could ask you the same question," he replied, looking a little sheepish.

"It's obvious what we're doing," Stevie replied. "We're riding. It's not nearly so obvious what you're doing. Does it have to do with your surprise?"

Max grinned. "You bet it does," he said. "Take another trail, please. This one is closed."

"Well," said Lisa as the girls and their horses went back across the wet edge of the field, "I wonder what that was about."

"If we wait a few minutes," suggested Stevie, "we can sneak back—"

33

"No." Carole interrupted her friend. "If Max sees us back there, he might not let us do whatever it is he's planning. There are plenty of other trails to ride."

They turned away from Pine Hollow and entered the woods in a different place. The fresh spring breeze had dried up much of the mud, and the horses walked confidently and happily. The air smelled sweet.

Stevie took a deep, appreciative breath. "This is my favorite part of riding," she declared. "My absolute favorite part."

"I thought it was dressage," Lisa said.

"No," Stevie said simply. "Dressage is my favorite competition riding—my favorite stuff to do in a ring. This is real riding, out here. Remember all the neat trail rides we've had? The mountain rides and the bareback rides at dawn?"

Carole and Lisa nodded. "Being out in the open on a horse," Stevie continued, "is the best thing in the world. It makes you feel *free*."

"I agree," Lisa said. She reached forward to give Prancer a pat. Prancer had a wild streak because of her racehorse breeding, but even she seemed to find the trails calming. They rode in silence for a while.

"I wonder if Emily has ever ridden on a trail," Carole said suddenly.

The three girls looked at one another. "Do you think

she could?" Lisa asked at last. "It can be a lot harder than riding in a ring. If the horse decides to run, there isn't a fence or anything to stop it."

"And it takes more balance, and more strength, because the ground is uneven," Carole said. "I don't know if Emily could do it."

"We haven't seen her ride," Lisa reminded her friend. "We don't have any idea what she can do."

"P.C. could do it, though," Stevie said.

There was another silence. Stevie's joy was not quite as complete as it had been. If she felt this free on a trail ride, she could imagine how free Emily, who could hardly walk, might feel. "She sure acted like she knew her way around a horse," she said.

Carole repeated, "We just don't know."

WHEN THEY CAME back from their ride, the girls dismounted outside the stable and walked their horses in the driveway to cool them off. They hadn't ridden fast, but the warm day and the horses' thick winter coats had combined to make the horses damp with sweat. They had to be walked until their coats were dry so that they wouldn't get chilled and then sick.

As Carole walked Starlight past the door of the indoor arena, she looked inside. Veronica was riding Danny alone over a grid of poles on the ground. Carole watched in appreciation as Danny naturally shortened and lengthened his trot stride over poles that were spaced different lengths apart. Veronica sat quietly on his back. She wasn't getting in his way at all, which was, Carole realized, the best way for Veronica to ride him. Danny knew how to do everything without any help from Veronica.

Stevie and Lisa brought their horses up beside Carole. "What're you watching?" asked Stevie. "Ohhh," she added when she saw Veronica. Veronica nodded curtly in The Saddle Club's direction, then turned Danny down the diagonal and let him lengthen his stride. His legs flashed forward, elegantly and beautifully. Veronica turned at the far end and rode him back across the other diagonal. This time she shortened him; instead of becoming slower, his stride became more upright, his legs moving up and forward with precision.

"I can't stand it," Stevie groaned. "She'll have that horse doing a *piaffe* next. It's not fair." The *piaffe*, an elevated trot in place, was one of the most difficult and advanced dressage moves. Only the most athletic horses could even attempt it.

"She's riding well," Lisa said reluctantly. "It's not like her to be here on a Sunday, though. She must be practicing for Max's surprise."

"Of course she is." Stevie's voice was bitter. "Miss Upper Class on her high-class horse. It'll be Danny's first show

36

since she got him, and Veronica wants to be sure they'll win so she can prove how superior they are to the rest of us. And I'm sure they will win. Look at that horse." Danny was cantering in beautiful balance and control down the long side of the arena.

"Don't be sure," Carole said gently. She laid her hand on Stevie's arm. Carole always wanted Starlight to do his best, but she honestly didn't care if his best was a blue ribbon. Stevie was much more competitive: She really wanted to win. Carole and Lisa sometimes felt Stevie wanted it too much. "You love your horse and she loves you. That counts for a lot. And Belle is a great horse, too."

"I know," Stevie said. She turned around and scratched Belle's forehead, and the mare lowered her head and sighed.

"Let's look on the bright side. Max said his 'event' was going to be different," Lisa reminded them. "He practically told Veronica not to count on winning."

"And she practically told everyone that she would," Stevie said. "I hope Max is right. I really hope I can beat her. I hope we all can. She's been way too superior ever since she got Danny. She needs to be taken down a peg or two."

"She sure does," Carole agreed. "Well, she does!" she repeated when her friends looked at her in surprise. "I'm with you, Stevie—let's beat her!"

On Monday afternoon Lisa's mother took The Saddle Club to Free Rein.

This time the horses were in their stalls and the stable was full of people—more than a dozen, by Lisa's quick count. Ms. Payne spotted The Saddle Club and came to greet them. "It's always a little hectic around here when lessons are going on," she said. "Pat, our regular instructor, is teaching a private right now. We've got three to get ready for the four-thirty lesson."

"Only three?" Carole was amazed. At Pine Hollow,

group lessons usually had six to eight riders, but even then there weren't nearly this many people in the barn.

"Three riders," Ms. Payne explained, "eight volunteers for the lesson, one instructor, two volunteers who are cleaning stalls, three parents watching their children ride, the three of you, myself—"

"And there's Emily!" Lisa spotted their friend outside P.C.'s stall. They waved, and Emily waved back.

"And Emily. That's, let's see—"

"Twenty-two people," Lisa supplied.

"That's right."

"Did you say eight volunteers for the lesson?" Stevie asked incredulously. "Eight volunteers for three riders?"

"That's right," Ms. Payne said again, nodding. "Some of our riders ride independently, the way you do, without anyone standing close by. Most require a leader; that is, a person who stands at the horse's head and leads it with a rope to be sure that it stays under control while the rider rides. Many also need side-walkers, who stand at the side of the horse and make sure that the rider doesn't fall off. For this lesson, two of the riders need two side-walkers, one on each side of the horse."

"And the third rider just needs one side-walker?" Lisa asked.

Ms. Payne sighed. "Well," she said, "I don't know if

Joshua really needs a side-walker at this point, but I don't know if he's ready to ride without one, either. It's hard to tell with Joshua. He's autistic. Come, I'll introduce you."

Joshua was twelve or thirteen years old. He was standing in a stall with a big-boned Appaloosa and two volunteers who were a little older than The Saddle Club. "We're going to groom Ditto now, remember?" one of the volunteers asked him. Joshua didn't reply. Physically he looked perfectly normal, as far as The Saddle Club could see, but he didn't seem to notice anything going on around him. He stood beside the horse, staring at it, and he didn't turn when they entered the stall.

"What do we do first?" the volunteer asked him. The boy didn't move. He didn't even seem to hear her. "Joshua?" The volunteer stepped in front of him and held up a grooming bucket. "What do we do first? Show me." Slowly, without looking at her, Joshua reached forward and touched the rubber currycomb. "That's right! Good!" Joshua turned his gaze back to the horse. The volunteer gently placed the currycomb in one of his hands, and he began to groom the horse.

"Girls, meet Joshua, Sarah, and Darcy," Ms. Payne said. "Joshua, Sarah, Darcy, this is Lisa, Stevie, and Carole. They're going to be helping us today. It's their first time helping with a lesson."

Ms. Payne left Carole with Sarah, Darcy, and Joshua. Carole watched as Sarah led Joshua through all the steps of grooming a horse. Joshua seemed to know exactly what to do, but he never did it until Sarah asked him to. His face remained expressionless. When Sarah sent him out to get Ditto's tack, Carole asked about him.

"Autism is strange and I don't really understand it," Sarah told her frankly. "It's something people are born with. Autistics typically have a great deal of trouble communicating with people, and they don't cope well with changes in their environment. Joshua seems to understand language, but he doesn't talk. He's never spoken to anyone in his life."

"Does he like riding?" Carole asked.

Sarah shrugged. "Who can tell?" she said. "No, that's not true. He must like it, or he wouldn't do it. But he never smiles or looks happy."

LISA FOUND HERSELF helping a small boy named Toby groom his horse. Toby had Down syndrome, but he knew everything about grooming. A volunteer named Sam peppered Toby with questions as they brushed a gray mare named Duchess. "How many legs does Duchess have?"

Toby bent over and counted. "Four!"

"Good! How many feet?" Sam asked.

41

Toby chuckled. "Four—that's silly. It's the same as legs."

"Yeah, Toby," Sam said. "Here's a hard one: How many shoulders?"

Toby paused and thought hard. *You can do it*, Lisa thought. "Two," he said at last.

"Good!" Lisa said. She wanted to try this herself. "How many of us are in this stall?" she asked him.

"Four," Toby said.

"Oh, no." Lisa felt unreasonably disappointed. "Three, Toby. You, me, and Sam."

Toby grinned. "You're wrong," he told her. "You, me, Sam, and Duchess. Four."

"You're right. I forgot Duchess," said Lisa, grinning back.

"I'm right, I'm right," Toby chanted happily.

STEVIE'S RIDER WAS a ten-year-old girl named Claire. She was developmentally disabled, like Toby, and she was blind. Her horse stood on cross-ties in the aisle. Emily had P.C. on the cross-ties just behind Claire's horse. Stevie greeted Emily and then got to work.

"Just watch for now," Wendy, another volunteer, said to Stevie. Claire couldn't reach very high, but her horse was small and she could groom most of it herself. To Stevie's surprise, Claire knew exactly what to do. She knew where the grooming bucket was kept on the shelf, she knew all of the grooming tools by feel, and she knew where and how to

42

use them on the horse. Claire kept both hands on the horse's side.

"Tell Stevie why you keep both hands on the horse," Wendy instructed.

"So I can feel the dirt, and so I can tell when the horse moves. I don't want to get stepped on."

"I don't want you to get stepped on, either," Wendy said. "What do we do if the horse moves?"

Claire laughed. "We dance with the horse! Stevie, we just dance with the horse."

"But no aerobics," Emily cut in from the back.

"Ballroom dancing," Stevie agreed. "Do you do a waltz, Claire? One-two-three, one-two-three—" Stevie could remember when Lisa had had to take ballroom dancing.

"A fox-trot," Emily supplied. Emily and Stevie cracked up.

"Hey, Emily," Claire said, "what's P.C. stand for today?"

"Peanut-butter Cookie."

DURING THE LESSON, The Saddle Club didn't do much except walk beside the horses, paying close attention. The experienced volunteers led the horses and made sure the riders didn't fall off, but the riders held the reins and told the horses which direction and how fast to go. Most of the lesson was at a walk, and most of the time was spent playing what The Saddle Club thought of as games.

First the riders walked their horses around a series of cones on the ground. Then they walked them over ground poles while standing up in their stirrups. They leaned forward in the saddle and touched their toes. They touched different parts of the horses' bodies. They threw soft foam-rubber balls at a basketball hoop. Finally, toward the end of the half-hour lesson, the instructor, Pat, had them trot one at a time.

"That's it, keep going, sit up!" she called as Toby bounced his way down the long side of the arena, the volunteers running alongside. "Fantastic, Toby!"

Stevie raised an eyebrow at Carole. Toby was grinning from ear to ear, but Stevie didn't think there was much about that trot that was fantastic. Carole raised her eyebrow back in seeming agreement.

"Your turn, Joshua!" Joshua seemed to be waiting for the command, because he quickly cued his horse to trot. He sat up straight, the reins looping from his hands. Stevie nodded. Joshua's trot was better. But still, his reins were too loose, his heels weren't really down . . . Stevie knew that if she'd ever looked like this, even when she was just starting out, Max would've told her to correct about eight hundred different things. "Good job! Try to keep your heels down next time," was all Pat said. Stevie wondered if this was really riding.

"Claire, how brave do you feel today?" Pat asked the little girl.

Claire looked toward Pat's voice. "Pretty brave," she said cautiously.

"Brave enough to trot?"

Claire's eyes widened. "Maybe," she whispered.

"What do you think, Claire? Is today the day?" Pat asked.

"Stevie!" Claire yelled.

Stevie jumped, startled. "I'm right here," she told Claire.

"Can you stand by my horse, too?" Claire asked in a quieter voice.

"Sure." Stevie moved closer to Claire's horse.

"Okay," Pat said, "you've got four people around your horse. You're not going to fall off. Are you going to go for it? *Ba-da-da-dum-ta-dum!*" Pat made a trumpet sound. "Ladies and gentlemen, this is Claire's first trot."

"Okay." Claire took a deep breath and urged her horse into a trot. She held on to the pommel of the saddle and bounced. Stevie remembered how awkward riding at a trot felt before she learned to sit to it properly.

"Just relax," Stevie told Claire. "You're doing great."

When Claire stopped her horse at the end of the arena, her whole face was lit with a triumphant joy. She leaned forward to hug her horse. "I did it!" she cried.

"Yeah, Claire!" Pat and all the volunteers cheered. "Fan*tas*tic!" This time Stevie agreed.

She and Lisa and Carole stood in the middle of the arena while the riders dismounted and led their horses to the stable. "That was really neat," Lisa said. "I was . . . I don't know, I was beginning to think that this wasn't like riding, but seeing Claire trot for the first time made me think that it was."

"Exactly," Stevie said. "At first I was judging these kids by what *we* could do. But that's not fair."

"It takes a lot of guts to trot on a horse you can't even see," Carole said. "Particularly if you don't know what a trot is like. Think about it, guys. Claire can't see anyone else trot, either, so she really didn't know what she was getting into. And the games they played did make sense. Don't you remember when we used to do things like that?"

"Remember?" Lisa laughed. "I still try to touch my toes sometimes. Max showed me how great it is for balance."

As they walked out of the arena, a man standing by the gate said, "Thanks for helping, girls."

"You're welcome," Carole replied. "Do you know one of the riders?" She hadn't seen this man volunteering.

"Toby's my son," the man replied.

"I helped him get ready," Lisa said. "He counted all the parts of the horse."

The man smiled. "That's because Toby is working on

46

counting in school right now," he said. "He has trouble with numbers. We told the instructors here, so they work counting into his riding to help reinforce his schoolwork. He's more interested in counting horse parts than anything else. Toby's a pretty big horse fan these days."

"That's neat," Lisa said.

"Riding helped him learn the days of the week, too," Toby's father said. "He knows he rides on Mondays, so every day he would ask, 'Is today Monday?' until he got all the days figured out."

"How long has he been riding?" Stevie asked.

"Three years."

The Saddle Club looked at him in dismay. Even Lisa, who had learned to ride last of all of them, had been able to trot and canter after only a few lessons. Toby hadn't learned much in three years.

"I can see what you're thinking," Toby's father said gently. "Girls, you may not realize what learning is like for someone like Toby. He takes very small steps. He's made enormous progress here.

"When he first started coming, he was afraid of the horses. He liked the way they looked, but he didn't want to touch them. Now he grooms them, plays with them—he even holds the reins himself when he rides. A lot of this self-confidence shows up at home and at school, too.

"The best part," Toby's father continued, "is that the

47

horse never judges him. The horse never thinks he's too slow, and the horse never makes fun of him. He can succeed here on his own terms. For Toby, riding is a secure joy.

"Anyway," he concluded, "I've never seen you here before, so I wanted to be sure to thank you for helping. It means a lot to Toby and me."

"You're welcome," Carole said again. She was immeasurably touched by all that Toby's father had said. "I didn't think that we were helping very much, but maybe we were."

"You certainly were."

"Whew!" Stevie said, as they walked into the barn. "I guess it was a pretty good lesson!"

THE SADDLE CLUB helped the riders untack and put their horses away. Emily was still there and, in fact, was almost tacked up to ride. P.C. had a saddle on.

"Do you have a lesson?" Stevie asked.

"No, I'm just riding," Emily said. "I've got a half hour before the next lesson starts in the ring."

"Can we watch?" Lisa asked. "My mom isn't picking us up for another twenty minutes. We'd love to see P.C. in action."

Emily grinned. "He's a Pretty Cool horse. Watch this." She tossed the reins in the air so that they came down over

P.C.'s neck, then unclipped the cross-ties. When P.C. held his head at normal height, his chin came just about to Emily's shoulder. Emily pulled a crop—a short, mild type of whip—off the grooming shelf and gently stroked P.C.'s cheek with it. P.C. dropped his head to his knees. Emily, leaning against his neck, began to bridle him with both hands.

"When I'm standing up, I can't lift both my hands in the air and still keep my balance," Emily explained. "I used to have to ask someone to help me bridle my horse, but when I got P.C., I taught him this." P.C. held his head down until Emily rubbed his cheek again.

"That *is* pretty cool," Stevie said. "I've seen horses that were taught to shake hands and do other tricks, but this is the first trick I've seen that was actually useful."

Emily led P.C. into the arena. "Maybe one of you could help me," she suggested. "Usually I ask Pat to do it."

"Sure," said Lisa. "What should we do?"

"Just hold P.C. by the mounting ramp for me. He's good about standing still, but it takes me a long time to mount and I worry about something spooking him. I could fall between him and the ramp, and I don't want that to happen."

"Okay." Lisa held P.C. while Emily made her slow way up the ramp. At Pine Hollow there was a standard mounting block outside the main ring. It was a wooden cube

49

about three feet high, with steps on one side. A rider with a horse that was too tall to mount from the ground led the horse to the block, climbed the steps, and got on from there.

Free Rein had a mounting ramp instead of a block. The top of it was the same height as Pine Hollow's block, and there were steps, with a handrail, on one side; but on the other side a long, shallow ramp led to the top.

"I don't do steps," Emily said when she was about halfway up. "I can't lift my feet very high."

Finally Emily made it to the top. She took off her leg braces, hooked them and her crutches over the ramp's top rail, and gathered P.C.'s reins in her hands. She grabbed the saddle with both hands, slid her left foot into the stirrup, then leaned forward and carefully slid her right leg over P.C.'s back. She found her right stirrup and sat up.

"Thanks," she said. Lisa moved away.

Right from the start, they could see the difference between Emily in the saddle and Emily on the ground. She sat tall and proud, her heels down and her head high. She held the reins with authority. Moving P.C. to the rail of the indoor arena, she asked him to trot, then grabbed his mane and picked up her two-point position, her seat slightly out of the saddle.

"I always do this, to give him a chance to warm up his

back," she explained. Carole nodded. She always did the same thing.

Emily trotted P.C. in circles and figure eights, then cantered twice around the ring, still in her jumping position. She brought P.C. back to a trot and began to post. Carefully, steadily, she smoothed his trot into a quieter rhythm. Emily's face was a study of concentration and happiness.

Carole looked at Lisa, who looked at Stevie. Stevie nodded and grinned. "Hey, Emily," she said. "Would you like to come on a trail ride?"

EMILY BROUGHT P.C. to a square halt in the center of the indoor arena. "Do you mean it?" she asked. Her eyes shone and her cheeks turned pink.

"Of course we mean it," Stevie replied. "There are tons of trails around Pine Hollow. We were talking yesterday about how we wished you'd come out there with us."

"I'd love to," Emily said. "I've never been on a trail even once. I've never been out of a ring. I'd really love to."

"You'd probably want to bring P.C.," Carole suggested. "We've got a lot of nice horses at Pine Hollow, but still—"

"Oh, I'll have to take him," Emily agreed. "Before I got P.C., I used to ride all the different horses here, but now I'd definitely rather ride him than anyone else. Besides, I can't not let him go on a trail ride! He'll enjoy it as much as I will." Emily thought for a moment. "Free Rein has a horse van, and my mom knows how to drive it—she trailered P.C. here when we bought him. I'm sure we can borrow the trailer, and I'll get my mom to bring us."

"We'll have to ask Max," Lisa said. "He's our director, and he always wants to know before we bring someone new over to ride. But he won't mind. He's really nice." Lisa dug a scrap of paper out of her pocket and Carole dug around in her own pocket and handed Lisa a pen. "I'll write down your phone number and give you all of ours," Lisa said. "We've got a lesson tomorrow. We'll ask Max then and call you."

"Super."

They heard a car pull up outside. Stevie peeked out the window. "That's your mom, Lisa," she announced. Lisa hurriedly finished writing the phone numbers and handed them to Emily.

"We'll see you soon," she said.

"I hope so," Emily said. "It sounds great." She gave P.C. a little tap with her crop and began trotting as The Saddle Club left.

AFTER THEIR LESSON the next day, The Saddle Club cooled out, groomed, and fed their horses, just as they always did. Then they cleaned their horses' stalls. Then they each

53

cleaned their own tack—which was usual—and one other horse's tack besides—which was not as usual. Then Stevie raked the aisle, Carole checked and filled all the water buckets, and Lisa straightened the locker room and swept the floor.

Everyone did chores at Pine Hollow, but eventually Max couldn't help but notice their extra efforts. "Ladies, I'm really impressed," he said, coming into the locker room where the three of them were cleaning out their cubbies. "I haven't seen you work this hard since—when? The time you painted Diablo red?"

"Oh, Max," Carole groaned. She hated the memory of that day. The Saddle Club had been trying to paint the front of the stable, but most of the paint had ended up on one of the horses. "That was a long time ago."

"Or maybe the time you wanted tickets to the American Horse Show?"

"You gave us those tickets," Lisa said severely. "We didn't ask for them. We always work hard, you know that."

"I do know that," he agreed, his eyes twinkling. "I'm very appreciative, believe me. Yet I can't help but think that I might somehow be able to repay you for all the work you're doing today."

"As a matter of fact," Stevie said, "there is one small thing—"

"Only a small thing," Lisa said. "Very small."

"You've let us do it before," Carole added.

Max sat down on a bench and crossed his arms. "If all that's true," he asked, "why all the extra work? Why are you trying to butter me up?"

"It's really important to us," Stevie answered.

"Okay," said Max. "Fire away."

"We want to ask a friend of ours to come here for a trail ride," Lisa explained.

Max laughed. "Let me guess," he said. "This friend is a boy, right, Lisa? A cute boy, but he doesn't ride very well—"

"No!" Lisa felt herself blush. So far, the boys she'd admired had all ridden very well, but that was beside the point.

"Emily rides at Free Rein," Carole said. "She has cerebral palsy."

Max's grin faded into an expression of sympathy and understanding. "Oh, girls," he said at last. "Oh, I just don't know. I'd like to say yes, but I don't want anybody to get hurt."

"Max," Stevie said, in an uncharacteristically firm and sensible tone, "you know we wouldn't have asked you if we didn't think Emily could do it. Please."

Max looked at them all for a long minute. "Okay," he said. "Come to my office. Let me see what Debbie Payne thinks about this."

55

Apparently Ms. Payne thought The Saddle Club's idea was okay, because when Max hung up, he looked less worried. "Do you know Emily's phone number?" he asked them. "I'd like to speak with her mother, too."

Lisa handed it to him. "Use the speaker phone," she suggested. "Please."

Max smiled at her and pushed the speaker button on the telephone. They could all hear the phone ringing at Emily's house.

Finally someone answered. "Hello?"

"Emily?" Stevie asked. "Emily, hi, it's Stevie. And Carole and Lisa. We're at Pine Hollow, and Max wants to talk to your mom."

"Hi, Stevie! Just a second." Emily put the phone down. "Hello?"

"Mrs. Williams?" Max introduced himself as the director of Pine Hollow.

"Oh, yes." Emily's mother laughed. "I'm glad you've called," she said, "because Emily hasn't talked about anything but this trail ride since she came home last night."

"I just spoke with Debbie Payne," Max said. "She feels that Emily rides well enough and isn't likely to be frightened by being out of the ring, and she says Emily's horse is as steady as they come."

"I'm not worried about Emily," Mrs. Williams replied. "Well, yes, I am, it's a big step for her, but we've always

56

encouraged her to be independent and try new things. She's very eager to do this. But tell me about these new friends of hers. Are they responsible? Can we trust them not to take silly chances? I know how girls this age can be." Mrs. Williams was apparently not aware that The Saddle Club could hear every word she said.

Max winked at The Saddle Club. "These three are the most responsible young women I know," he said proudly. "I'd trust them in any situation."

Stevie felt her face grow hot. She could personally think of several situations that Max couldn't trust her in. She was sure Max knew about at least some of those situations. On the other hand, she knew and Max knew that she never did anything stupid on horseback. Max was right. There was no fear that Stevie would hatch one of her schemes while riding with Emily.

Max and Mrs. Williams talked for a few more minutes, and then Emily came back on the phone. They arranged to meet at Pine Hollow at nine-thirty Saturday morning.

"That'll give us plenty of time to groom, tack up, and have a nice long ride before lunch," Carole said. "We've got a Horse Wise meeting at one o'clock."

"Horse Wise? Is that your Pony Club?"

Carole remembered that Emily had said Pony Club sounded like fun. "That's right, it is," she said. "We're just having an unmounted meeting this week. I think Meg and

Jasmine are giving a presentation on polo wraps. It's not going to be a big deal, but maybe you could stay for it. We always have a picnic lunch here on Saturdays. Would you like to?"

"Really?"

"Of course really," Stevie cut in. "Four is a much better number for lunch than three. The sandwiches divide more easily."

"I'll bring dessert," Emily said. "Does your mare like bananas?"

"As a matter of fact, no," said Stevie. "I tried them on her once, and she didn't like them at all."

"P.C. doesn't like them either," Emily said. "So I'll bring something, but not bananas."

They hung up the phone and Max began to laugh. "I can't wait to meet her," he told Stevie. "She's the first person I've ever talked to that reminded me of you!"

THE SADDLE CLUB walked into Pine Hollow Stables and stopped dead, staring. It was Saturday morning. There in front of them was Dr. Dinmore, the old woman they'd helped put on Patch last weekend, and she was grooming Calypso!

Calypso was a beautiful Thoroughbred mare that Max had bought especially for breeding. Like most Thoroughbreds, she was high-strung and skittish, and she was rarely used for lessons. "Oh, Dr. Dinmore!" Carole said, advancing with an air of command. "You really shouldn't have taken that horse out of her stall!"

"She can be a little frisky," Carole explained. She gently

took Dr. Dinmore's arm and guided her out of harm's way. Lisa and Stevie returned Calypso to her stall.

Dr. Dinmore watched them with mild amusement. "Mrs. Reg told me that I was going to ride Calypso," she protested.

Stevie raised an eyebrow. "Calypso? She couldn't have meant *Calypso*."

"That's what she said." Dr. Dinmore was wearing a different elegant white shirt, this time with a bolo tie, over a pair of fancy leggings. She didn't look any more like a rider than she had the last time. "I'm sure Mrs. Reg said Calypso. She's in the office—she just got a phone call."

"She must have said something that sounded like Calypso," Lisa decided. "I'm sure she wouldn't let you on Calypso. No offense, but Max doesn't let any of us ride Calypso! How about Diablo? Could it have been Diablo?"

"Or Delilah?" Carole suggested. Delilah was a very sweet palomino mare. "I bet it was Delilah. She's down here." Carole started to walk toward Delilah's stall, but Dr. Dinmore didn't follow.

"Last time you told me to ride that old plug Patch," she said. "I think maybe you girls don't understand what I want."

Carole frowned, considering. A lot of people who didn't really ride attached too much importance to a horse's looks, or to the color of its coat, or to whether or not it was

60

a purebred. Carole knew that those things could be important in certain limited situations, but that what mattered
most about a horse was that it had a willing heart. Patch
had a good heart, but he was sometimes more lazy than
willing.

"Delilah can be easier to ride than Patch," Carole admitted. "Patch is very gentle, but Delilah listens a little
better. And she's a mare—do you like mares?"

"I like Calypso," Dr. Dinmore replied.

"Come meet Delilah," Carole offered. "I'm sure you'll
really like her when you see her."

"We'll show you how to groom her," Lisa said helpfully.
She started to gather the tack Mrs. Reg must have gotten
out for Dr. Dinmore.

"Where's your hard hat?" Stevie asked, looking around
the area. "Don't forget, you have to wear one."

"I wouldn't forget a thing like that," Dr. Dinmore assured her. "But girls, as much as I appreciate your eagerness
to help—"

"What are they doing this time?" Mrs. Reg asked, coming out of the office. Her eyes narrowed a bit when she saw
The Saddle Club clustered around Dr. Dinmore.

"We're helping," Stevie explained. "Dr. Dinmore misun-
derstood and thought you wanted her to ride Calypso."

"We told her Delilah would be a better choice," Carole
added.

Mrs. Reg's eyes narrowed a bit more. "Why?" she asked. "Come to that, why Patch last time? Why shouldn't she ride Calypso?"

"Because—" Stevie thought about it and shut her mouth before the rest of the sentence escaped. She'd been going to say, "Because Dr. Dinmore is so old." Mrs. Reg was probably at least as old as Dr. Dinmore. Stevie had a feeling that Mrs. Reg wouldn't appreciate being called old.

"Because we knew you wouldn't want to frighten her when she's just starting out," Lisa cut in. She could see what Stevie was thinking. She didn't think they needed to remind Mrs. Reg about her age, either, but she knew that they were doing the right thing. Lisa had never ridden spirited horses until she had taken lessons for long enough to know what she was doing most of the time. Starting out quietly was the right way to learn to ride, and Lisa was sure that Mrs. Reg would be happy they were so conscientious.

Mrs. Reg didn't look happy. She didn't look unhappy, either; she looked like she was trying to stifle either giggles or stomach gas. "I won't frighten Dr. Dinmore," she said. "I promise you that. But I'll assign the horses, okay?"

"Okay." The Saddle Club looked at one another, shrugged, and went to get their own tack. They were only trying to help. Normally Mrs. Reg was more appreciative.

Before they got all the way to the tack room, they heard Mrs. Reg ask Dr. Dinmore, "Do you *feel* like a fossil?" Both women exploded into laughter. The Saddle Club didn't understand it at all.

The girls groomed their horses thoroughly and hung their tack near the horses' stalls so that they could get ready quickly when Emily came. They finished just in time to see a big blue horse trailer pull up in front of the stable. Emily waved from the front seat, and her mother came around to help her climb out of the cab. Emily wore paddock boots and breeches underneath her leg braces, and she already had her hard hat on her head. Lisa and Carole unloaded P.C. while Stevie introduced herself to Emily's mother.

P.C. stepped out of the trailer and looked around eagerly. The new sights and sounds seemed to interest but not overexcite him. Lisa handed Emily P.C.'s lead rope and went back to help Carole unload his tack, water bucket, and other gear. The four girls said good-bye to Emily's mother and headed for the stable.

"Just a minute." Emily's mother reached into the cargo hold of the trailer and pulled out a folded manual wheelchair. She snapped it open.

"Oh, Mom!" Emily sounded horrified.

"Em, you might want it," Mrs. Williams said, kindly but firmly. "You know you get tired, and this is going to be a long day. It will be worse if you need your chair and don't have it than if you don't need it and do have it."

"Not much," Emily muttered, but she asked Stevie if there was somewhere they could hide it in the barn. Stevie wheeled it into the locker room while Carole and Lisa showed Emily an empty stall she could use for P.C.

"Before I started riding, I had to use that stupid wheelchair all the time," Emily said as she snapped P.C. onto a set of cross-ties. Pine Hollow didn't have a handy shelf for Emily to put her grooming tools on, but Stevie moved a hay bale over for her to use. "All the physical therapy in the world wasn't enough to make me walk. These crutches aren't so bad compared to using a wheelchair all the time."

"Is riding really that good for you?" Lisa asked. "It feels like my legs are a little stronger now that I ride, but I never really thought of riding as something you did to build muscles." She went into Prancer's stall and began to saddle her.

Emily brushed P.C.'s coat hard. "Riding's great," she said emphatically. "The thing is, when you sit on a horse, its movement naturally causes you to kind of sway back and forth, right?"

Lisa turned and nodded. Even when riders looked as if they were sitting perfectly still on a horse, they weren't. They had just learned to move in harmony with the horse's movement.

"Well, that swaying exactly mimics the way your hip and leg muscles move when you walk," Emily said. "Horseback riding is the only therapy that moves your muscles in the same coordinated way as walking—and the horse does the moving for you. You don't have to be able to move at all. Even paralyzed people get better muscle tone and flexibility. Some of the people at Free Rein have to be held on to their horses. Instructors ride double behind them and keep them upright. They don't hold the reins or anything. Some of them have a doctor's prescription saying they need to be on a horse for so many hours a week."

"I didn't know that," Lisa said.

Emily moved to the other side of P.C., out of Lisa's sight. "I'll tell you about therapeutic riding," she said, "you tell me about the trails. Where are we going to go?"

The Saddle Club's descriptions of all the interesting spots in all the trails around Pine Hollow lasted until they were ready to ride. Then came a problem none of them had thought of. Lisa, Carole, Stevie, and Emily led their horses outside the stable, since all of them knew better than to mount in the low-ceilinged aisle. Emily saw Pine Hollow's small, square mounting block, and her face paled. "Whoops," she whispered.

The Saddle Club looked and realized exactly what she meant. "Could you use it if we helped you?" Stevie asked. They walked over to it and tried, but Emily couldn't lift her foot high enough to clear the first step. Stevie and Lisa tried to help her, but the steps weren't wide enough to accommodate more than one person at a time, and Stevie and Lisa couldn't push her up the steps. Carole held all four horses, who were getting nervous.

"What if I gave you a leg up?" Stevie asked. She had often helped boost some of Pine Hollow's smaller riders into the saddle.

Emily shook her head. "I don't think you could," she said. "I can't jump, I couldn't help you, and I weigh too much for you to lift me all the way onto P.C."

"We'll figure something out," Stevie assured her.

Just then the girls saw two familiar figures: Red O'Malley, Pine Hollow's head stable hand, walking out of the stables, and Veronica, the head nuisance, pulling up in her Mercedes.

"Let me," Red said quietly. He picked Emily up in his arms, lifted her high, and gently set her down on P.C. Emily, her face red, began to fumble with her leg braces. "I'm sorry," Red said, "I should have asked if you wanted those off first, shouldn't I?"

"It doesn't matter," Emily said. "Thank you very much." She looked very embarrassed. Stevie undid the second brace and hung both of them on the fence rail. Emily got her feet into the stirrups, and The Saddle Club mounted, too.

As if mounting alone hadn't been embarrassing enough for Emily, Veronica watched it all open-mouthed through the window of the Mercédes. She stared at Emily as though Emily were purple and green and riding a donkey. Stevie turned in the saddle and glared back at her while they rode away, but Veronica was talking to her chauffeur by then and didn't seem to notice.

As soon as they were away from the stable, Emily's embarrassment vanished. She drew a deep breath of the fresh spring air and looked around appreciatively at the open fields. "We're going to take the path along the creek," Lisa informed her. "There's a rock where we have picnics sometimes, and we want you to see it."

"Most of the trail is flat, and in many places it's wide enough that we can ride four abreast," Carole added. "It's really a pretty trail. How do you feel so far?"

"Great!" Emily looked totally at ease. The Saddle Club had carefully arranged it so that when they were riding single file, Carole led on Starlight. Emily rode next, then Stevie and Lisa. They didn't want P.C. to feel that he had to compete with too many horses, and Starlight was a steady leader. When they rode side by side, they were sure to keep Emily in the middle.

The first spring wildflowers were starting to bloom. The air blew softly through the leafless branches and the short, newly greening grass. It was, Stevie decided, as nice as any trail ride she had ever been on. Part of the joy was being able to share it with Emily.

"Does P.C. feel nervous at all?" she asked. "He looks great."

"Placid and Calm," Emily said, laughing. "He's P.C."

They took a winding path through the woods until they got to the edge of the river. There was a wide, smooth place there, and Carole tentatively suggested that they try a trot. Emily agreed wholeheartedly. P.C. pulled ahead, steady and quiet.

"Good boy," she said to him, pulling him up where the trail began to narrow again.

"I saw you use your crop on him when we started trotting," Carole said. "I use mine to get Starlight's attention when he's ignoring me, but I know P.C. wasn't ignoring you. Do you use it for a different reason?"

Emily nodded. "You might have noticed me using it when I was riding at Free Rein, too," she said. "I always do. I sit comfortably in the saddle, but I really can't use my legs the way you guys do. I can hold them still, but I can't signal my horse with them—not very well, anyway. So I use my crop, not to punish P.C., but to tell him what to do." She laughed. "I call my crop my third leg," she said. "It works better than my other two."

"That's really neat," Carole said. She was always interested in horse training. "Did P.C. understand that when you got him, or did you train him yourself?"

68

"Neither. My parents and I looked for a very well trained, quiet, happily obedient horse, and then we had him trained some more so that he would be good for me. The farrier who comes to Free Rein trains horses on the side, and he rode P.C. and got him used to being signaled with a crop instead of leg commands. Then the instructors at Free Rein put him through the training program they have for all the therapeutic horses—getting him used to the mounting ramp, getting him used to being whacked by my crutches—"

"Getting him used to girls falling between his legs . . . ," Stevie supplied, grinning.

"Exactly. It only took him a few months to learn everything. He's so good."

"He doesn't mind that you don't use your legs?" Carole asked. Carole had always thought of her legs as her most important aid. She couldn't imagine not being able to use them when she rode.

"No, he doesn't seem to," Emily said. "We knew it could be done. I know a girl—well, she's almost a grown-up now, —but she rides regular dressage and she only has one leg. She had cancer and they had to amputate the other. And there was another dressage rider from Denmark, back in the 1950s, named Lis Hartel. She got polio and was permanently paralyzed from both knees down. Then she won two

69

individual silver medals at the Olympics. She's the reason the whole therapeutic riding movement eventually began."

"Olympic dressage?" Carole knew she sounded incredulous, but she couldn't help it. "Two silver medals and she couldn't even feel her feet?"

"Cool, isn't it?" Emily said. "I read that the gold-medal winner had to help her stand on the podium."

"Is that why you like dressage?" Lisa asked.

"I like it for all sorts of reasons," Emily answered. "I like the way it looks, and I like the way it feels. I like the way you have to really understand horses in order to do it well. And, yeah, I figure if Lis can do it, so can I."

They rode for nearly an hour before turning back. When they reached a wide part on the trail, Emily suggested a canter. The Saddle Club was happy to agree. All of their horses were behaving well and they deserved a little chance to move out.

When they got back to Pine Hollow, they saw Red lingering near the gate of the outdoor arena. Since he was usually very busy on Saturdays, The Saddle Club guessed that he was waiting to help Emily dismount. They were right. Red carefully lifted her down, helped her fasten her braces, and handed her her crutches before shyly going back to his work.

"He's really sweet, isn't he?" Emily asked them as they watched Red disappear into the stable. "All the same, I

70

wish I didn't need his help." The Saddle Club nodded understandingly.

They led their horses into the stable. Veronica was grooming Danny in the aisle. It amazed The Saddle Club to think that she had been working on him for as long as they had been riding, because Veronica was better known for neglecting her horses than fussing over them, but apparently that's just what Veronica had been doing. She'd pulled Danny's mane and neatened his tail, and she'd cleaned him from the tips of his freshly trimmed ears to the edges of his polished hooves.

Stevie felt disgusted. How could any of them beat Veronica and her megahorse when Veronica was trying this hard to win? No matter what Max's competition was going to be like—and Stevie was very eager to hear the details—Veronica looked like a shoo-in. The rest of them might be competing for second place.

"Pretty is as pretty does," Carole hissed in Stevie's ear. Startled, Stevie turned to Carole and smiled at the look of understanding on her friend's face. She knew Carole was right. But Danny performed well, too.

Emily politely asked Veronica to move Danny to one side, so that she could get past with P.C. Veronica did so, but grudgingly. "Be careful!" she shrieked, as Emily's crutch missed Danny's hoof by an inch. "You're scaring my horse!"

71

Emily pressed her lips together and kept moving. The Saddle Club could see that Emily hadn't scared Danny at all. In fact, the only thing that appeared to make him nervous was Veronica's screeching.

"What are you doing letting someone like that come here?" Veronica said next, talking loudly to The Saddle Club with both hands on her hips. "What'd you do, put her on a pony and walk her around the back paddock? Really! I thought that the whole purpose of that other place was so that people like her wouldn't have to come here!"

The Saddle Club was appalled. They had always known Veronica was a jerk, but now she seemed to be taking her jerkiness to a new low. Even discounting what she was saying, she was talking about Emily as if Emily couldn't hear.

Emily looked over her shoulder. "Isn't it amazing," she said in the same loud, rude tone that Veronica had used, "how some people can have a whole lot of money and still have absolutely no class at all?" Like Veronica, she spoke directly to The Saddle Club, as if Veronica weren't standing right there. Emily winked.

Taking their cue from Emily, The Saddle Club marched their horses past Danny without saying a word to Veronica. When they got to the other end of the aisle, Stevie congratulated Emily. "You knew exactly how to deal with her," she said. "I'm glad you figured her out so quickly."

"There's a moron in every crowd," Emily said. "Unfortunately, I'm used to it."

"Unfortunately," Lisa agreed, "we're used to Veronica. Come on! Let's have lunch!"

THE SADDLE CLUB and Emily had a pleasant lunch on the hillside behind the stables. Samson and some of the other horses played in the pasture below. "This is so nice," said Emily, stretching out on the grass. "I wish we had this much space at Free Rein. I'd love to ride outdoors all the time."

"Me too," Lisa said. "I'm grateful for the indoor arena when the weather is bad, but I'd much rather be outside."

"When I'm jumping indoors," Stevie confided, "I always feel like I'm going to hit my head on the ceiling!"

The others laughed. "The ceiling must be forty feet

above your head!" Carole teased her. "You couldn't hit it if you grew wings!"

"I know," Stevie said, grinning apologetically, "but that's how I always feel."

THEY MADE A POINT of getting back to Max's office early so that Emily could find a seat in a chair instead of having to sit on the floor for the Horse Wise meeting. The room became crowded early. Most of the riders chattered excitedly about Max's surprise, and he didn't disappoint them.

Toot-to-da-doo! Max blew on a hunting horn as he came in the door. *Toot-to-da-doo!* He strode to the front of the room and unrolled a small paper banner. It read in black marker: THE FIRST ANNUAL MAX REGNERY JUNIOR HANDY HUNTER TRAIL COMPETITION! The riders read it in silence. Then Lisa raised her hand.

"I understand 'First Annual Max Regnery,'" she said. "That's obvious. Same with 'Trail' and 'Competition.' And I understand 'Junior,' that's any rider under eighteen. A 'Hunter' is a horse that jumps low fences with good style, the way a foxhunting horse should. But what's a 'handy'?"

Max grinned. "Anyone have a guess?" he asked.

Carole thought hard. "A horse that's really listening to its rider is said to be *in hand*," she said. "Is that sort of what it means?"

Max nodded. "That's right. Handy hunter classes aren't

75

seen very often in horse shows these days, but they used to be quite popular. They usually involved a course of fences, like a regular hunter course, but with some special instructions—for example, sometimes you had to trot over a fence instead of ride it at a canter, or halt and back up a few strides before continuing. Then there would be special obstacles, too—you might have to open a gate from horseback, ride through it, and close it again. You might have to ride your horse through water or over a bridge. The emphasis was on a horse that obeyed his rider at all times, under any circumstance, the way a true hunter should."

"And that's what we're going to do?" asked Stevie.

"Sort of," Max said. "I've changed the concept a little, because I wanted to have a single competition that would be fair to all of you. Some of you younger kids haven't been jumping very long, for example, and it's really not fair to put you up against, say, Carole and Starlight."

Carole smiled softly with pride. The younger kids looked glad that they wouldn't be jumping against Carole, and Veronica looked annoyed that Carole had been mentioned instead of her.

"But all of you should be able to get your horses to obey you," Max continued. "That's the first rule of riding, the first thing you start to learn—how to make your horse listen, and make it glad to do what you want. I don't mean to say that obedience is easy to come by, but it's something all of you should be working on all of the time.

"So here are the rules," he said, putting down his banner and picking up a notepad. "First, this is a trail competition, because I thought that would be fun. You'll start off one at a time, like in a cross-country jumping competition, only you'll stay on one of our usual trails."

Lisa grinned. So that was what Max had been doing with the tractor!

"Second"—Max tapped his notepad—"at various spots along the trail—ten spots, in fact—there will be stations manned by a pair of judges. At each station you and your horse will have to perform a particular handy hunter-type test.

"Third, you're not going to know ahead of time what any of the stations are going to test. You'll ride up, and then the judges will tell you what to do.

"I'm emphasizing horse-and-rider teamwork," Max continued. "Remember that. You might have to cross a creek or open and close a gate, as I already described. You might have to trot your horse over a crossrail, a small log, or some other very small fence—nothing that all of you can't do— and you'll be judged not on how prettily you ride or how stylishly your horse takes the fence, but on how calmly your horse approaches and negotiates the fence.

"You might be asked to dismount and remount your horses. You might be asked to walk in and out through a gridwork of ground poles, or walk your horse backwards between a pair of straw bales.

"Think real-life riding skills," Max concluded. "There'll be a prize for first place, and ribbons for the top six. Are you interested?"

A resounding cheer answered his question. The Saddle Club exchanged excited looks. Max was right—it sounded like fun! Lisa leaned forward to whisper to Stevie and Carole, "You-know-who isn't necessarily a shoo-in. I've never seen Danny walk through water."

Stevie grinned. "Neither have I. He walks *on* water, according to Veronica, but he might not go through it." Many horses didn't like to get their feet wet. Stevie, Carole, and Lisa had been on so many trail rides that their horses didn't mind creek crossings at all.

"We could beat her at this," Carole said. "But don't forget Max's point—what's important here is how well we communicate with our horses. That's always the most important thing."

"That, and beating Veronica," Emily put in. "I hope you all do!"

The Horse Wise meeting continued with Meg and Jasmine's presentation. The whole group trooped out of the office to watch Jasmine wrap her pony's legs while Meg explained why and how polo wraps are used. Then the whole group trooped back in.

Trooping was not easy for Emily. Looking at her, Lisa realized that Emily was getting tired. Lisa was almost glad when the meeting was over.

"Stevie," Max said as Horse Wise filed out the door. The Saddle Club and Emily were waiting for the crowd to clear so that it would be easier for Emily to maneuver. "I haven't met your friend yet. Is this Emily? How was the trail ride?"

"Fantastic!" they answered as one. They stood talking to Max for a few minutes. By the time they left the office, Veronica had already taken Danny to the riding ring just outside the stable doors.

"Wow!" Emily stopped and stared at Danny. "He really is a nice horse, isn't he?" She and The Saddle Club walked out to the edge of the ring.

Veronica was making Danny walk forward, back, forward, back. She turned him on the haunches and on the forehand, then began a serpentine at a canter, with flying changes of lead. Veronica was concentrating hard. The Saddle Club felt despondent. Clearly, Veronica was out to win the handy hunter competition.

"That's a beautiful horse!" Emily said to her. "You're really riding him well—look how nicely he's bending!"

The Saddle Club was a little surprised that Emily would praise Veronica. None of them would have, even though Emily's compliments were true.

Veronica brought Danny to a square halt. "Thank you," she said, looking down at Emily with a smug expression. "I'm so glad you could see him. You know, this is what *real* riding is all about."

Stevie moved closer to Emily. "Let's go," she whispered. "She isn't going to change."

Veronica either didn't hear or pretended not to. "You might want to come watch us compete next weekend," she continued. "It'll all be real riding—a lot different from those pony rides they take you on at Free Rein."

Emily flushed red. "I ride," she said.

Veronica smiled. "I'm *sure* you do," she said. "You should try to come next weekend. Then maybe you'd understand."

"Come on," Stevie whispered fiercely, her hand on Emily's elbow. "Don't listen to anything she says."

Emily nodded and turned back to the stable, but The Saddle Club could see that their friend's eyes were full of tears.

THE SADDLE CLUB and Emily retreated to the stable, united by their hatred of Veronica. "I know you were trying to be nice to her," Carole said, "and I think that's really admirable, especially considering how rude she was to you earlier. But trust me, it isn't worth the effort. She's so sure she's right that she'll never change."

Emily slumped onto a hay bale and pulled her arms out of her crutches. She wiped at her eyes. "I just wish she hadn't said that about my riding. I really do ride."

"We know." Stevie sat down on the hay bale next to her friend.

Lisa reached into her pocket. "The only cure I know for

Veronica's kind of poison is chocolate," she said. "Hot fudge. I've got ten bucks my grandma sent me for Valentine's Day. Can I treat you all to a hot fudge sundae?" The Saddle Club looked at one another, then at Emily. "Emily?" Lisa asked.

Emily looked up, and the bitter look in her eyes surprised them. "Even kids with C.P. like hot fudge," she said.

"Oh, no," Lisa said, in genuine alarm, "that's not what I meant at all. The ice cream store—TD's—is about half a mile from here. Do you think you can walk that far?"

Emily gave a short laugh. Her expression brightened, but barely. "I guess my stupid wheelchair is good for something," she said. "Let's go!"

The Saddle Club took turns pushing Emily in her wheelchair along the shoulder of the road. They were a little surprised at how difficult it was. The wheelchair rolled easily enough, and on smooth ground any one of them could push it one-handed, but on gravel and dirt the wheels caught and it became much more unwieldy. They had to dodge discarded soda cans and potholes, and they couldn't walk along the grass the way they usually did. When they reached the edge of Willow Creek and the sidewalks started, they had trouble getting Emily's wheelchair over the steep curb. The trip to TD's seemed to take much longer than usual.

Worse, Emily seemed very depressed. She hardly spoke, even when they asked her questions. A gloomy silence descended on them all.

Stevie felt horrible. It had been her idea to ask Emily to come to Pine Hollow! She really wanted Emily to have a nice time, and now it seemed that Veronica was spoiling everything. Stevie wished she could say something to make Emily feel better. She wished she had a super-death ray to blow Veronica off the face of the planet.

At TD's they sat at a table instead of their usual booth so that Emily could pull her chair right up to it. Emily looked around the ice cream parlor with more interest than she had shown on the way there. "Cool place," she said appreciatively. "What's that smell?"

"They bake their own chocolate-chunk brownies," Stevie said. "I'm going to have a brownie sundae, with pistachio ice cream, strawberry sauce, peanuts, and a maraschino cherry."

Lisa and Carole watched to see how Emily would react to this. Stevie was famous for her strange ice cream concoctions. Neither Lisa nor Carole understood how Stevie could eat them, but she always did. Emily raised her eyebrow, as if thinking about Stevie's order, but she didn't say anything.

Their usual waitress came up to their table and nodded in a friendlier-than-usual fashion. Lisa and Carole ordered hot fudge sundaes. Stevie ordered a brownie and pistachio sundae, just as she'd described.

"I'll have a brownie sundae, too," Emily announced. "Only I'll have mine with lemon sherbet, caramel sauce, and some of those neon Gummi Bears sprinkled on top. Oh, and a maraschino cherry."

Stevie's jaw dropped open. Carole and Lisa stared. The waitress stopped smiling. "Another one!" she muttered to herself, and stalked away.

"What?" Emily asked. "What'd I do?"

Stevie snapped her jaw shut. "Nothing," she said. "I knew we had a lot in common."

The waitress brought them glasses of water. Lisa played with the paper wrapper on her straw. "Emily," she said tentatively, "we're sorry about Veronica. We're sorry anything had to happen today to make you feel uncomfortable."

"We really wanted you to have a nice time," Carole added. "We wouldn't have invited you otherwise."

Emily smiled ruefully. "You don't need to apologize. I'm not upset with you guys. And I'm sorry, too. I'm sorry I sulked. I *was* sulking.

"I'm used to walking slower than everybody else," she continued, "and I'm used to crutches and wheelchairs, and curbs that are too high—none of that bothers me too much. But I can't get used to attitudes like Veronica's.

Plus, what she said really hurt." Emily leaned forward. "There are a lot of things I can't do," she said emphatically, "but I know I can ride. *Really* ride." The waitress brought their sundaes, and Emily leaned back so that hers could be set in front of her. "I'll get even with her," she concluded when the waitress had gone.

"How?" Stevie's ears perked up. Getting even was her specialty.

"Don't get mad, get even," Emily said. "That's what my father always taught me, ever since I was a little kid. He doesn't mean that I should actually get revenge on anybody, he just means I should work really hard, so that I know the person who insulted me isn't right."

Emily took a big brownie–lemon sherbet–and–caramel sauce bite. Carole tried not to look.

"Like, instead of believing Veronica," Emily continued, "what I'll do is focus on how well I can ride. I'll work harder in my lessons, and I'll concentrate on how much I can learn if I keep trying. I'll think about what I can do, instead of what I can't."

"We-ell," said Stevie, considering, "that sounds fine, but I think revenge would be nice, too."

Emily took another bite. "I totally agree," she said around a mouthful of brownie.

Carole started laughing. "You two really are birds of a feather!"

85

Lisa scraped her spoon around the rim of her dish to catch some drips of hot fudge. "What kind of revenge?" she asked practically.

"What if we stick a pin in Veronica's saddle?" Stevie suggested. "When she goes to mount, it'll stick her right in the—"

"Not negative revenge," Emily objected. "Positive."

"Like showing Veronica how well you can ride," said Lisa.

"Like showing everyone how well you can ride," said Stevie.

Carole laid down her spoon and spoke very softly. "Like riding in the handy hunter competition."

Emily beamed. Lisa let out a long sigh.

"That's it!" Stevie said. "That's perfect!"

"I'd love to," said Emily. "Wow, would that be cool."

"It'd show Veronica," Lisa said.

"Particularly," Carole added, "if dear P.C. beats Danny."

"I don't care about that," Emily said quickly. "I probably won't even be able to place, but just finishing—just trying, even—that would be like a victory. It would be a victory to me."

The four girls finished their sundaes in silence, thinking hard.

"Do you think I can do it?" Emily asked at last.

"Of course," Stevie said promptly. Lisa and Carole nodded.

"We'll help," Carole offered.

"Whatever help is necessary," Lisa said, and they all
smiled. On their trail ride, they had told Emily about The
Saddle Club and its rules.

"We've got a whole week until the competition," Stevie
said. "That's ages, compared with how much time I've had
to plan other things."

"I ride every day at Free Rein. I'll be able to spend a lot
of time practicing."

"We'll come there and help you get P.C. ready," Carole
said. "We can set up some obstacles in the ring like the
ones Max described."

"Maybe you can bring P.C. to Pine Hollow next Friday
and take another trail ride," Lisa suggested. "We know
Max'll let you do that, and we'll ask him about the handy
right away."

"No," said Stevie. The other three looked at her. "No,
Lisa, not right away. We're not going to go back to Pine
Hollow and say, 'Max, Veronica was mean to Emily, so
she's going to ride in the handy.' Think about how that
will sound."

Lisa grimaced. "You're right," she said. "Max won't
really understand. He'll think we're just—"

"Whining," Stevie concluded. "Going off half-cocked. Remember, I've got a lifetime's experience dealing with three brothers and sibling warfare. What we need to do is work on our own until we're all the way ready. Then we'll tell Max."

"I'll wait to tell my mother, too," Emily said, agreeing with Stevie. "She's not as into revenge as my father is."

STEVIE'S PARENTS WERE lawyers, so they had conference calling on their home phone. Stevie used it later that night to call the rest of The Saddle Club and Emily all at once.

"Time to talk strategy," Stevie said. "Let's think about what Max said we'd need to do at the stations on the trail. Then we can think about how to teach P.C."

"He said he wasn't going to tell us exactly what the stations were," Emily said.

"Yes." Lisa thought hard. "But Max is fair, and he wants us to listen to him, so what he says is usually important. He gives out a lot of hints. The stations probably won't be exactly like what he said, but if we know how to do what he said, we should be in good shape."

"P.C. really felt comfortable on the trail," Emily offered.

"He looked comfortable," Carole agreed.

"Practically Comatose," continued Emily. The Saddle Club laughed.

"If you come over on Friday, we can practice creek cross-ings," Carole said. "But he didn't seem spooked by being near the stream today."

"He wasn't. I don't think that walking backward or for-ward through any kind of obstacle is going to bother him, either. We do a lot of that at Free Rein already, and he's used to having all kinds of crazy stuff around him. I mean, there's even a basketball hoop in the arena. It's the jump-ing that's worrying me."

"Can you hold your two-point position at a trot?" Carole asked. Stevie snorted. Sometimes Carole already sounded like a riding instructor.

"Yeah, if I grab mane," Emily said. "Remember? I did it in the ring when you were watching me. That's how P.C. and I warm up."

"Then you'll be able to jump okay," Carole assured her. "It's only going to be a single fence, and the hardest part about jumping is putting all the fences in a course together. Plus, whatever you might jump has to be small enough for the little kids to clear it easily on their ponies, and P.C.'s a pretty good-sized horse. He'll probably even be able to step over the fence. All we'll have to do is teach him to get to the other side."

"We can do that," Emily said. "He learns fast."

"How about opening a gate?" Stevie asked.

"Will I be allowed to use my crop?"

"Sure," Stevie said. "I use mine when I open a gate from horseback. It isn't hard. I'll show you."

"Sounds great."

"Uh-oh," Lisa said.

"What?" asked the other three at once.

"I just remembered something else Max said. He said he might make us dismount and remount our horses."

There was a moment of dead silence as each girl remembered Red lifting Emily onto P.C. that morning.

"That's a stupid test," Stevie said angrily.

"No, it isn't," Carole replied. "I'm not trying to argue with you, Stevie, but it's in the horse show rule book as one of the tests judges can ask even very young riders. Every rider ought to know how to get on and off her horse properly. It's a fair test."

"But I can't do it," Emily said. "Not without a ramp."

The sadness in her voice made Lisa's heart sink. "Maybe Max won't ask that one," she suggested.

"If he does I'll be disqualified," Emily said.

"Wait!" Stevie cut in suddenly. "I've got an idea!"

"IT'S THE GIRLS from Pine Hollow!" Ms. Payne sounded delighted to see them. "I talked to Max over the weekend—he told me you call yourselves The Saddle Club. Is that right?"

"That's right," Stevie said, speaking for all of them. "We told Emily we'd help her work on a few things with P.C. But we'd like to help out with the other lesson first, if that's okay."

"Sounds great, girls." Ms. Payne smiled warmly. "I'm glad you're here. Why don't you help the same riders you helped last week?"

They went into the stable. Emily wasn't there yet, but

Carole paused to pat P.C. before she looked for Joshua and the volunteers helping him. Joshua rode a different horse this week, but he hadn't changed. He didn't look at Carole, not even when she spoke to him, and he didn't make a sound. He did a thorough job of grooming his horse, however, and he put on the saddle without help. Carole watched him a little sadly. She wondered if they would ever know whether he liked riding. She wondered if Joshua even knew.

TOBY WAS HAVING trouble counting. "How many hocks?" Tom asked him as Lisa joined them in the stall. This was a hard question, Lisa realized, because it meant that Toby had to understand what hocks were as well as be able to count them.

"Three," Toby guessed. Lisa knew it was a guess, because horses were symmetrical—all their parts came in pairs. They didn't have three of anything.

"Show me a hock, Toby," Tom suggested. Toby correctly pointed to the bottom part of the horse's leg, what Lisa might have described as an ankle before she started riding. "Good! How many hocks?"

"Five," said Toby.

"Four," Lisa stage-whispered.

"Four," agreed Tom. "Let's count them together, Toby: one, two, three, four."

92

"Four."

"Okay, Toby, here's an even harder one. How many hairs on the horse?"

Toby looked at Lisa, a big grin on his face. "About a bazillion," Lisa whispered.

"About a bazillion!"

"Hello, Claire," Stevie said as she came up to the little girl. "It's me, Stevie."

Claire turned her face in the direction of Stevie's voice. "Who's Stevie?" she asked.

"I helped you last week." Stevie tried not to feel disappointed. She'd only met Claire once, after all.

"Stevie's my friend," called out a voice Stevie knew.

"Oh, hi, Emily!" Claire knew Emily's voice, too. "What's P.C. stand for today?"

"Politically Correct," Emily answered, grinning at Stevie.

Claire frowned. "What's that mean?"

"Never mind," Emily said.

Carole continued to watch Joshua throughout the lesson. Once, just once, she thought she saw the expression on his face change—he didn't smile, but for an instant he looked lighthearted. Carole was glad.

Claire trotted without being afraid, and Toby correctly

counted the number of strides his horse took on the short side of the arena. It was a very good lesson.

EMILY HAD FULLY tacked P.C. by the time the lesson was finished. Lisa held P.C. near the ramp while she mounted, and Stevie and Carole pulled some ground poles and used them to outline an L-shaped pattern in the center of the ring. Emily warmed P.C. up at a trot and a canter. Then she asked P.C. to walk through the L. He did it happily.

Emily halted him and asked him to walk backward through the L. This was harder: Most horses don't like to back up, because it makes them nervous not to be able to see where they are going. P.C. listened to Emily carefully and backed through the L obediently. The Saddle Club was especially impressed with the way he swung his hindquarters over when Emily tapped them with her crop.

"When I tap him high on the hip, it means 'over,'" Emily explained. "When I do a sort of fluttery thing behind my leg, that means 'trot,' and a firmer tap behind my leg means 'canter.'"

"Let's try a more complicated figure," Carole suggested. She set up a sort of open cross. Emily rode P.C. into the middle, and from there they could go in any one of three directions. P.C. had to listen to Emily instead of choosing a route on his own. Again, he did very well, walking both backward and forward.

94

Emily patted him and let him trot around the ring a few times to reward him for concentrating so hard on the patterns. Meanwhile, The Saddle Club used a pair of small stepladders to create jump standards in the center of the ring.

"Walk him through the standards first," Carole told Emily. "See if they bother him."

They didn't. Next, Carole set a pole on the ground between the standards. P.C. stepped over it solemnly. "We do a lot of work over poles," Emily told them. "He knows to walk over them, and he doesn't get nervous."

They added poles on either side of the stepladder standards so that P.C. had to walk over several of them. While he went through them, Emily held herself in her two-point position. After P.C. had walked through the poles several times, Stevie and Lisa stuck one end of each of two poles through the first rungs of the stepladders. The other ends of the poles lay on the ground. They formed a very flat X shape. The middle of the X was only a few inches off the ground.

"This is called a cross rail," Lisa explained. Emily walked P.C. over the low center part. It didn't seem to bother him.

"Good boy!" Emily said. She stroked his neck. P.C. tossed his head. Stevie thought he looked proud of himself.

Carole removed the ground poles before and after the tiny jump and had P.C. step only over the jump. Then she threw her red ski jacket over the jump to make it look different and told Emily to walk P.C. over that.

"What if he steps on your coat?" Emily asked.

"It won't be the first time a horse has stepped on that coat," Stevie assured her on Carole's behalf. "I've seen her do the same thing for Starlight."

Carole pretended to be offended. "Starlight would never step on a jump!" she said. "He's much too surefooted."

P.C. didn't step on Carole's coat, either. He did snort a little and roll his eyes at it, but Emily pressed him forward calmly, and in the end P.C. went over the coat and rails willingly.

"That's enough jumping practice for now," Carole finally said. "We don't want P.C. to get tired, and we've got a lot yet to do." She glanced over at Stevie, who was humming to herself. Carole thought Stevie's plan might work, but she wasn't as convinced of it as Stevie and Emily seemed to be.

"We should try opening the gate first," Emily suggested. "From what you told me, that might be hard for me to do, so I need to start practicing."

To open a gate while on horseback, a rider first had to ride her horse alongside and very close to the gate, so that the gate's latch was near the rider's leg. The rider reached down and unlatched the gate; then, holding on to the gate, the rider asked the horse to move forward, pushing the gate open at the same time. Then the rider asked the horse to pivot so that the horse would be facing the other direction but his forelegs would still be in the same place. The rider asked the horse to walk forward while pushing the gate closed, and finally she moved the horse's side against the gate in order to reach down and latch it.

It was a tricky maneuver and could be very difficult if the horse wasn't patient or didn't want to walk forward into the gate. When The Saddle Club went on trail rides, they all practiced opening gates, but more often one of them just hopped off her horse and held the gate open for the others. Out West on Kate Devine's ranch all of the horses were steady gate-openers. Belle was pretty good at it, and Carole could do it on Starlight, but Lisa still struggled when she tried it with Prancer. Lisa often thought that Prancer would rather jump the gate than wait for Lisa to open it.

Stevie explained the gate-opening to Emily in detail, then explained it again step by step while Emily and P.C. tried it with the arena gate. As Emily suspected, it was harder for her than for P.C. P.C. waited patiently while Emily fumbled with the latch, and he didn't flinch when Emily lost her grip and the gate hit his chest.

"I'm sorry, P.C.," Emily muttered. She tried again. After

several attempts she managed to walk him through the open gateway, but she couldn't pivot him while still holding the gate. She needed one hand to use her crop to ask P.C. to turn, and she needed the other hand to hold her reins. She didn't have a hand left to hang on to the gate.

"I need three arms," she said, shaking her head at The Saddle Club.

"What if you held on to the very end of the reins, and held your crop in the same hand?" Lisa suggested. "You could use your crop without pulling on P.C.'s mouth."

Carole objected. "If he decides to run off, she'll have no control holding her reins like that."

"If he decides to run off while I'm hanging on to a stupid gate, I'm history anyway," Emily said. "I'm just barely keeping my balance as it is. Anyway, I can't use my crop. I need to use it behind my inside leg, to get him to pivot away from it, and I need to hold the gate with that hand. I can't hold the gate with my outside hand."

"You're going to have to," said Stevie, after studying the problem. "Either that or use your inside leg to get him to move."

Emily frowned. "I can't use my legs."

"You're going to *have* to," Stevie said.

"I *can't.*"

Lisa and Carole looked at Emily sympathetically, but

Stevie crossed her arms and looked disdainful. "Isn't the whole point of doing this proving what you *can* do?" she asked. "Just push your ankle into his side and think, 'Move, P.C.'"

Emily looked ready to spit fire. "Easy for you to say," she said to Stevie.

Stevie looked Emily straight in the eye. "No, it isn't," she said.

Emily blinked. "Okay," she said. "I'll try it. Easier, maybe, than holding the gate in the wrong hand." She took a deep breath and grabbed the top of the gate again. She clucked to P.C. and he walked forward. "Whoa," she said to him softly when he was clear of the gateway. P.C. stood. Emily tried to move him sideways. He didn't move. Emily grimaced. Sweat broke out on her forehead.

"C'mon," Lisa whispered, "you can do it." She wasn't sure if she was talking to Emily or to P.C.

Emily took a deep breath and tried again. P.C. took a step sideways. The Saddle Club cheered. P.C. put his ears back and stopped. Emily relaxed and gave him a small pat with the hand she held the reins in. She was still holding the gate, bent forward in cautious balance. "One more step," Emily said as if to herself. She concentrated hard, and P.C. gave a sigh and moved his hind legs over.

Emily dropped the gate and the reins and slouched on

P.C.'s neck. "Good boy," she crooned to him. To The Saddle Club she said, "That's enough of that for now. I'll try it again later."

"If you can do that, you can do anything," Stevie said, her eyes shining bright. "This dismount and mount is going to be a piece of cake. Now, here's what we need to do. . . ."

ON FRIDAY AFTER SCHOOL Emily brought P.C. to Pine Hollow for another trail ride. It was a beautiful day. From a distance, some of the underbrush was even starting to look green, as tiny leaves began to unfurl.

The Saddle Club groomed their horses quickly. Carole felt a slight pang of regret that she had not spent more time with Starlight in the past week. She'd ridden him on Tuesday, in their usual weekly lesson, and she'd come to Pine Hollow to groom him every day before she left for Free Rein, but she hadn't had time to ride him.

She knew Red had turned Starlight out in the pasture to graze and play, so the horse had gotten enough exercise, and Carole certainly didn't regret spending the time with Emily. They'd done so much in one week! Plus, Carole had learned how much she enjoyed teaching others to ride. She'd always been helpful around the stable—sometimes a little too helpful, she knew, because other people didn't always want her advice—but she'd never taught anyone with special needs before. It had been fun, and it had been satisfying. Still, she had missed Starlight. When she grew up, if she decided to teach riding, at least she wouldn't have to go to school. She'd have plenty of time to spend with her own horses.

Lisa combed Prancer's mane. She'd missed riding too, partially because she loved it so much, but partially because she knew she wasn't as prepared as the rest of The Saddle Club for the next day's competition. Lisa hadn't been riding for as long as Carole and Stevie. She knew she'd learned fast, but her reflexes still weren't as sharp as her friends'. Prancer was also the least experienced of the three horses. *Oh, well,* Lisa said to herself. She'd learned long ago to compete for the joy of doing well on her own terms. Like Emily, Lisa hoped to ride as well as she could. She wasn't worrying about blue ribbons this time.

Lisa thought back to the evening before, when Emily had finally managed to open, walk through, and close the gate at Free Rein. "Victory!" she'd shouted, throwing her hands in the air, and The Saddle Club had crowded around

P.C., patting him and clapping Emily on the back. It had been a terrific moment.

Stevie hummed as she curried Belle's shining flank. For once in her life, she wasn't worried about beating Veronica. At least, not personally. She couldn't wait until the next day's competition.

All three girls heard the Free Rein horse trailer rattle up the bumpy driveway. By the time they got outside, Emily's mother was already leading P.C. out of the van. Emily was climbing out of the cab.

The Saddle Club stopped short. Fresh from grooming their own horses, they could see how really raggedy P.C. looked by comparison. His winter coat was thick and shaggy. He still had a patch of mud on his rear, behind the saddle, and dust hung around him.

"He rolled in the paddock today," Emily said, sounding very exasperated. "My mom helped me groom him and tack him up before we came. It took us forever, and he still looks horrible! He had mud all over, he was disgusting—I'll never have time to get him clean by tomorrow."

"What's tomorrow?" Mrs. Williams asked.

"Nothing, Mom, I'll tell you later. Okay? Thanks." Emily kissed her mother and took P.C. from her. Mrs. Williams gave Emily a slight frown, shook her head, and got back into the cab of the trailer.

"She knows something's up, she just doesn't know

what," Emily said. "She told me she'd be back in an hour and a half. We've got to hurry!"

They started out on the trail. This time, The Saddle Club took Emily on a slightly more varied route. "Max isn't letting anyone ride on the trail for tomorrow's course," Stevie said. "He's already got the stations up, and he doesn't want anybody cheating. But we can show you all the different kinds of trails."

They rode up hills and down. They rode in fields of dead grass, in deep, muddy woods, and across short stretches of gravel. They took P.C. across several streams. As Emily had predicted, he didn't seem to mind the water at all. In fact, he even seemed to enjoy it.

At one point a small log lay across the path. Carole went over it at a trot and turned Starlight to watch Emily, who was next. Emily balanced P.C. and brought him to a walk. He came up to the log and neatly hopped over. Emily praised him soundly. "He's having a great time," she declared. "He's going to do fine."

The Saddle Club exchanged smiles of happiness and relief. It did look as though P.C. would be fine. "If only—" Lisa began.

"Hush," Stevie told her firmly. "We don't want to talk about it. We might jinx things."

"No talk," Emily agreed. "I don't need to be any more·

nervous than I already am. Let's head home. I don't want to make my mom mad by keeping her waiting. Not now."

Lisa looked at Emily. She didn't look nervous. Like Stevie, Lisa found she couldn't wait until morning.

EMILY ASKED HER MOTHER to come into Max's office. For a moment the four girls only looked at Max and Emily's mother, not saying a word.

"Out with it," Max said encouragingly. "I know that look," he told Mrs. Williams. "They want a favor, and they don't think they're going to get it. Girls, what is it?"

"I would like to ride in the handy hunter competition," Emily said, with characteristic suddenness.

"Oh. Well." Max's smile dimmed and he seemed at a loss for words. "Well, now—"

All the girls talked at once.

"She can do it, Max!" said Stevie.

"We've been working with her every day," Carole added. "You know we wouldn't ask if—you said you trusted us—"

"It's a very simple competition," Lisa told Mrs. Williams, though she knew that wasn't completely true. "Max designed it for beginning riders. Emily really can—"

"I can do it, Mom!"

Max held up his hand. "Enough!" he said. The office went quiet. "Did you know anything about this?" he asked

Mrs. Williams. She shook her head. "It's a little competition I planned for my Pony Club," Max explained. He went on to give the details of the junior handy hunter trail competition. "It's true that I planned it with my beginning riders in mind," he concluded. "Everyone from Pine Hollow should be able to complete the competition safely, though only the good and more experienced riders are going to do well. But I don't know about your daughter—I worry about whether it would be safe for her."

"It doesn't hurt me to fall off any more than it hurts Lisa or Carole to fall off," Emily said hotly. "I'm not fragile. I don't break."

Max looked at Mrs. Williams. "That's true," she admitted. "There's nothing about cerebral palsy that makes falling off any more dangerous for Emily than for anyone else. But still—"

"But still," Max echoed. Turning to Emily, he said, "This class is going to be run one rider at a time, through the woods. You may not be more likely to get hurt if you fall off, but I think you are more likely to fall off on a trail ride than an able-bodied rider."

"Not on P.C.," Emily protested.

"I know you've come here and ridden," Max said, as if she hadn't spoken. "I know you've done well, and I know you have a fine horse. But I'm not comfortable with the idea of you going down those trails alone, considering the very limited experience you've had with them. I can't let you ride in the trail class. I'm sorry." He looked sorry.

"Max," Lisa asked. "Is that really your main objection? You don't want Emily on the trails alone?"

Max nodded. "That's it."

"What if I rode—well, with her, on the course, but so my ride didn't count. There's a word for it, I read it in a horse magazine. 'Hors d'oeuvres?' That's not it." Lisa flushed. Hors d'oeuvres were foods like the deviled eggs and cheese spreads her mother served at bridge parties.

"Hor de concours," Max corrected her, smiling gently.

"You can't do that," Emily said. "Lisa, I can't let you! It wouldn't be fair to you or Prancer!"

"That's it," Lisa said, ignoring Emily. "Emily could go first, and her ride would count. I'll just ride Prancer along behind, and make sure she doesn't get into trouble by herself." Lisa shrugged. "Prancer wasn't likely to do too well at this anyway," she said. "Obedience isn't her strong point, yet."

"Well," Max said slowly, "if you're sure you want to—"

"Of course I want to. We've been practicing for this all week! It won't be any fun if Emily can't be with us."

"I can't let you," Emily said again, in a softer voice. She looked at Lisa with a worried frown.

"I don't mind," Lisa said. "Honest." She really didn't. Emily seemed to believe her, because she smiled.

"Safety really was my only objection," Max said. "If you want to ride with her, Lisa, I'll let Emily try it. But you have to promise me . . ." He turned to Emily. "You, Emily, have to promise me that you won't attempt any stations that are beyond your experience. Don't experiment on the trail!"

Emily nodded. "We've been practicing the stuff you talked about," she said. "But if something comes up that I don't know how to do, I won't try it."

Max turned to Mrs. Williams. "I told you before that I trust these three riders, and I do," he said. "How do you feel about this?"

Mrs. Williams looked at her daughter and shook her head, smiling. "Emily, you are so determined," she said. "I don't know, it seems like a lot for you to take on, but if you want to, I guess it's okay with me."

The girls whooped. Max smiled. "I wondered why I hadn't seen you riding all week," he said. "It didn't make any sense that my three most faithful riders would suddenly desert the stable just when they most needed practice. Now I understand."

Emily's smile disappeared. "Oh, gosh," she said softly. "I never even realized! None of you has been able to ride!"

"It doesn't matter," Carole said quickly. "We didn't care. We wanted to help you."

"But now you won't be able to beat Veronica! And Lisa,

you won't even be able to place! I shouldn't have let you!" Emily sounded distraught.

"I would rather come in last place behind you and P.C., and have Veronica beat us both, than win the whole thing without you riding," Stevie said in tones of utter conviction.

"And Stevie loves to win," Carole said with a laugh, "so you know she means it!"

"We're not doing this because of Veronica, or because we feel sorry for you," Lisa added, because Emily still didn't look convinced. "We helped you because you're our friend. I want to ride with you because you're my friend."

At last Emily smiled. "I'm glad that we're friends. But I still don't feel right about taking up all your time."

"We offered, didn't we? And look at it this way," Carole said. "Maybe because we helped you, none of us will be able to win, but *all* of us will be able to ride."

"Okay." Emily laughed. "Okay! What time should I be here in the morning?"

11

THE NEXT MORNING Pine Hollow was aflutter with excitement. Members of Horse Wise were grooming their horses even before Red had a chance to feed them grain. May Grover arrived with her pony, Macaroni, in her father's horse van, and several other Horse Wise members also trailered their own horses in. Every cross-tie and spare stall was in use.

The Saddle Club waited eagerly for Emily. Even though they had stayed late at the barn the night before, grooming, they had still arrived early in the morning. Carole had helped Lisa and Stevie trim their horses' muzzles, bridle paths, and ears. Lisa was amazed at what a difference the trim made in Prancer. She looked elegant and refined.

But not, Lisa realized ruefully, as elegant or as refined as Veronica's Danny. Veronica must have been working with Danny all week long, because only concentrated grooming would make a horse's coat shine so bright. Danny looked like liquid silver. His head was trimmed, his mane was braided, and his hooves were shining. Veronica's expensive tack shone with polish, and Veronica herself was elegantly turned out in gleaming boots and dove-gray breeches.

Lisa sighed. She knew that, at least in this competition, good looks weren't important. She knew that she and Prancer looked neat and clean. Still, she couldn't help being just a bit envious of Veronica.

"Hey! Lisa!" Lisa turned. Emily was waving from the entrance of the stable. "Where do I put P.C.? This place is packed!"

Lisa called Stevie and Carole over. "I'd like to stay out of her way," Emily added, pointing to Veronica.

"Good idea," Stevie said. "How much work do you have to do with P.C.?"

"Not much," Emily replied. "I put his saddle on before we got here. All I have to do is take him out of the trailer, take off his shipping wraps, and bridle him."

"Let's leave him in there for now," Carole suggested. "This place is kind of crazy. Max is going to explain the

111

rules in a minute, and then I bet all the little kids are going to get up on their horses. I've heard them talking—they all want to go first. We can wait until they clear out before we get ready."

Everyone agreed with Carole. The Saddle Club settled their groomed horses back in their stalls. "Starlight looks beautiful," Emily said admiringly. "And so do Belle and Prancer. The most I can say for P.C. is that he's clean."

They went to visit P.C. in his trailer. He thrust his stubby, shaggy head out the trailer door and whinnied to greet them. Emily rubbed his head affectionately, and Lisa fed him a carrot.

Then they heard Max call for order. They hurried to gather around him.

"Welcome to the First Annual Max Regnery Junior Handy Hunter Trail Competition," he began.

"Blow your horn, Max," yelled a rider in the crowd.

Max laughed, but he didn't have the hunting horn he'd blown during last week's meeting. "We'll get started here in just a few minutes," he said. "I understand that some of you"—he glanced meaningfully at May, Jasmine, and the other younger riders—"are quite impatient to be off. I'm going to send you out as I would for a cross-country course, one rider every four minutes. The course is timed. I have it set at a working trot pace, and if you go over the time allowed, you will incur penalties. The purpose of the time penalties is to reward those of you whose horses complete the stations quickly and move boldly down the trail, and to penalize those of you whose horses are hesitant. I do *not* want you racing down the trail. Do you hear me?"

"Yes, Max," they chorused.

"What did I just say?"

"No racing down the trail!"

"Very good," said Max. "Please, all of you, ride at the speed at which you are comfortable. If any of the station judges sees you riding in an unsafe manner, you will be disqualified.

"If your horse backs up in front of an obstacle, that counts as a refusal and will be penalized, just like in a regular horse show," he continued. "There will be ten stations on the trail, and two judges per station. The judges will give you penalty points for any faults your horse makes while it completes the station. The horse with the fewest accumulated points—the most perfect horse—wins."

"Well," The Saddle Club heard Veronica diAngelo say, "I think we know who that'll be!"

"Please be courteous and welcoming to our judges," Max said, ignoring Veronica. "Most of them are students in the state college's equine studies program, and all of them are volunteering their time.

"I'm especially pleased to introduce you to one judge who is *not* a student," Max concluded. "I've been very proud to have her riding with us for the past few weeks. Not only is she a noted breeder of quarter horses, but she's twice won the Mountain Centennial, one of the toughest endurance rides in the nation. Please meet Dr. Marian Dinmore!"

Dr. Dinmore stepped up to Max's side and waved to the crowd. She winked at The Saddle Club when she saw them. "I want to die," Stevie groaned.

"I told her to ride Patch," Carole said in tragic tones. "The Mountain Centennial! That's a race of over one hundred miles of mountain trail in a single day! It's one of the most difficult horse races in the world!"

"I offered to show her how to groom," Lisa remembered. She hid her face in her hands. "Oh, I'm so embarrassed."

"You wanted to show her how to groom?" Emily cracked up. "That's hilarious."

"She said she wanted to learn how to ride English," Carole recalled. "I just assumed she'd never ridden. I didn't even ask about Western riding."

Stevie shook her head. "We assumed a lot of things. We looked at her and decided that she didn't look like a rider, so she probably wasn't one."

"I bet you won't do that again," Emily said cheerfully. "Good thing you're not counting on winning this thing. Dr. Dinmore's going to be annoyed with you!"

114

But Dr. Dinmore was still watching them, and laughing. "She thinks we're funny," Lisa realized. "She and Mrs. Reg have been laughing at us all along."

"Better laughing than furious," Carole said. "Emily, we're not usually this stupid."

"I know. Good thing, huh?"

The little kids clamored to start, and Max began sending them off. Once the commotion around the barn eased a little bit, The Saddle Club found an open set of cross-ties and helped Emily bring P.C. inside. They tacked up their horses.

Of the four of them, Carole and Starlight headed out first. Starlight felt fresh and frisky; Carole was glad to be riding him, and she was always happy to have a chance to test his skills. She concentrated, and they did well. Toward the end of the trail, at the eighth station, she was asked to ride Starlight across a "bridge." This was really just several wooden planks, about six feet long, laid flat on the ground with hay bales on either side. The test was whether Starlight would walk calmly between the bales over a strange surface.

Starlight took one look at the planks and snorted. Carole patted him and walked him forward. Starlight snorted again, tucked himself together—and jumped the whole thing! He landed with his tail swishing, pleased with himself. Carole grabbed his mane when he jumped, and landed laughing. It was a pretty big mistake, but it was his only one.

Stevie went next. Belle caught the bit in her mouth and played with it. Stevie had more trouble settling her down than worrying about her going too slow. But once the obstacles began, Belle concentrated better, and she did well, too. Stevie's worst moment came during the creek crossing, when Belle stopped and began to paw the water with her foreleg. Splash! Splash! Stevie was drenched.

"Move her forward!" one of the judges cried. "She's going to roll!" Stevie urged Belle out of the water. The judges were laughing, and so was Stevie. Belle had never acted that way before, but it was funny. Stevie was very glad that Belle hadn't rolled. It was much too cold for a dunking.

Veronica headed out just before Emily and Lisa, who came out of the stable as Veronica and Danny were riding away. Red appeared beside them and helped Emily into the saddle.

"Ready?" Max asked, consulting his watch. "You're off!"

As arranged, Emily took the lead on P.C. She urged him into a fast trot. They knew that Emily was likely to be slow through some of the stations. She would have to make up time on the trail to avoid penalties.

"Don't go faster than you want to," Lisa called to her. Prancer was moving beautifully.

116

"I want to go faster than this!" Emily called back. "I want to gallop—I feel like I'm flying!" But she stayed in a trot.

They trotted through the field that had been wet two weeks before. It was much drier now. At the far end of it was the first station: a gate.

"Uh-oh," Lisa murmured.

Emily shook her head. "I'd rather get it over with early," she said. The gate had a wire loop closure rather than a chain and hook like the gate at Free Rein. This made it a little easier for Emily to grasp. She held it, and P.C. pushed the gate open. Then, while Lisa held her breath, P.C. pivoted in response to Emily's leg. Emily shut the gate, dropped the loop in place, and raised her fist to Lisa in triumph. Lisa grinned and raised her fist back. She opened the gate, sent Prancer through, and went after Emily without bothering to close it. Glancing over her shoulder, Lisa could see the jump judge frowning as he shut the gate. But Lisa couldn't stop to explain—Emily was already trotting.

Next P.C. jumped a hay bale and crossed the creek without fuss. He stepped neatly through a V-shaped figure and waited patiently while Emily retrieved a fake letter from a fake mailbox and handed it to the judge. He went calmly down a short stretch of steep downhill and stepped over the pole that was laid at the bottom. Lisa, following closely, watched the two of them with growing admiration.

Emily was as tough as nails, and P.C. was doing everything she asked.

Emily checked her watch. "Let's make up a little more time," she suggested.

"Fine," Lisa said. "This is the flattest part of this trail." They cantered until the next station. This was a difficult one: The judges asked Emily to back P.C. through an S shape laid out on the ground with a garden hose.

Lisa watched as Emily calmly switched her crop from one hand to the other, making P.C.'s hindquarters move from side to side the way they needed to. They didn't make a mistake through the S. They hadn't made a mistake yet.

P.C. walked calmly over the bridge that Starlight had jumped. He went up, over, and down a tiny banked jump. Emily looked back over her shoulder as she trotted him away. "That's the ninth station. Maybe they won't—"

"Don't be so sure," Lisa said. "I know Max."

They came out of the woods very close to Pine Hollow and trotted along one of the pasture fence lines. There in front of them was the final station. Because they had made up so much time, they could see Veronica still there. It was the dismount and mount.

Lisa realized how clever Max had been to put this station last. It was a simple task for almost all of the riders, except those too short to mount easily, but by putting it so close to the stable he had made it much harder. The horses would be impatient to get home. They wouldn't be expecting their riders to dismount at the edge of the woods.

Veronica halted Danny smoothly. She dropped her feet from her stirrups, put both reins in her left hand, swung her right leg over the cantle of the saddle, and dropped to the ground in a crisp show dismount. She all but saluted the judges.

Danny mouthed his bit eagerly, looking toward the stable. As Veronica placed her foot in the stirrup to mount, Danny took a step forward. It was a small error, but it was still an error. Danny was not perfect after all.

Emily walked P.C. into the station. Lisa stood behind her and held her breath. This is what they'd worked so hard for.

Emily brought P.C. to a square halt before the judges. She put the reins in her right hand and rested that hand against the crest of P.C.'s mane. With her crop, she gently reached forward and pressed the side of P.C.'s neck.

P.C. sank to his knees.

He lay perfectly still. Emily carefully dropped her feet from their stirrups and ever so slowly slid her right leg across P.C.'s back. Balancing herself on his neck, she stood.

Emily added the flourish that Veronica had not. Drop-

119

ping her right arm straight to her side, she dipped her head to the judges in the slow, elegant salute of a world-class dressage rider. She was grinning from ear to ear.

Lisa found herself nearly shaking with excitement. Emily bent forward and eased her leg back across P.C.'s back. She nosed her feet into the stirrups. P.C. still didn't move.

Emily gave him a brief hug before patting his neck again with her crop. He rose with all the grace of a circus elephant, and Emily trotted him across the finish line, her head held high.

"Wa-*hoooo!*" squealed a rider. Lisa recognized the voice; it could only be Stevie. She saw Stevie and Carole standing at the finish line, cheering. Several other riders were cheering, too.

"Under the time allowed!" Max announced, a giant smile on his face. Lisa wondered if he'd seen Emily's dismount. "Good for you!" Max said. Lisa concluded that he had. She trotted Prancer toward home, giddy with pride for her friend.

THE SADDLE CLUB and Emily sat still on their horses just outside the stable. All around them the other Pony Clubbers laughed and chattered, but the four girls were too happy to talk. Emily stroked P.C.'s neck over and over, her face aglow.

"They're a long time getting the results together," Stevie said at last. "I saw Max go out with the hay wagon and pick up all the judges."

"It probably takes a while to count up everyone's faults," Carole suggested. "How many faults do you think we got for jumping the bridge?" She absentmindedly played with Starlight's mane. She was proud of him—he had tried hard. She was proud of herself, too, and of her friends. No matter what the official results were, they had all done well. Emily's ride had been her own, but Carole had helped to teach her.

"All the judges are talking about something," Stevie said, looking over to where the final station had been. "They're waving their hands around. It looks interesting." She clucked to Belle and rode over to eavesdrop. Soon she returned with a grin on her face.

"They're talking about you," she said to Emily. "They're trying to decide if what you did was a legal dismount. The best part is, none of the judges knew you were disabled! The ones at the last station couldn't figure out why you made your horse lie down, and none of them knew why Lisa wasn't completing all the stations."

They laughed. "Max is explaining it to them," Stevie said.

"I'm glad he didn't tell them ahead of time," Emily said. "I wanted them to mark me fairly."

"Marian—Dr. Dinmore—she's taking Emily's side pretty strongly. She said, and I quote, 'She got on and off her horse, didn't she? You ought to give her double credit— triple credit—for being able to make it lie down. No other rider here could do that!'"

"No other rider here is riding P.C.," Emily pointed out. "I'm so proud of him. I can't even tell you how much. I don't care if they do disqualify us. Just being able to ride, and everything we did—that was enough. I'll never forget what this horse did today."

"We'll never forget what you did," Lisa said softly. "P.C. was awesome, but so were you."

Emily began to respond, but Stevie shushed her. "Here comes Max! He's announcing the results!"

Max stepped up to the microphone he'd placed near the gate of the outdoor ring. "Horse Wise, come to order," he said. "Testing—one—two—three . . ." All around the ring, the riders quieted and stilled their horses.

First Max thanked everyone for riding. He told them how proud he was of all of them. He thanked the judges again, and thanked Red, Mrs. Reg, and Deborah, his wife, for helping him put the competition together.

"And now"—Max ruffled the papers he held in his hand—"the moment you've all been waiting for." He paused and looked around the ring until a few of the riders started to grumble impatiently. "The moment you're all still waiting for . . ."

"Great, give him a mike and he becomes a comedian," Stevie muttered. Her stomach was tied in knots.

"I'm pleased at how well you all did," Max continued at last. "Many of you encountered trouble at some of the stations, but you persevered and all of you ultimately got your horses through. Well done!"

"He means there were some major refusals, but no one fell off," Lisa interpreted. The others grinned but didn't respond. They were too eager to hear what Max had to say next.

"Here are the top six, the ribbon winners, in reverse order of finish. In sixth place, Carole Hanson and Starlight!"

Carole rode Starlight into the ring and gracefully accepted her green ribbon. She was happy to get any color ribbon at all. She halted Starlight at the far end of the ring and waited for the others.

Max announced May in fifth place and Polly in fourth. "Third place—Stevie Lake and Belle!" The Saddle Club cheered. Stevie rode in proudly.

"Cross your fingers," Lisa whispered to Emily.

"They've disqualified me, I know it," Emily replied. "I'm not even going to think about it."

"Second place—Veronica diAngelo and Go For Blue!"

"Go for red, more like," Emily whispered, referring to the color of the second-place ribbon. Lisa was too busy watching Veronica to reply. From the look of utter, devastating astonishment that washed over Veronica's face, Lisa knew that Veronica had been expecting to win. She and Danny must have had a very good round.

"Veronica?" Max asked. Veronica remained motionless on Danny, gaping. "Would you like to come into the ring?"

124

Veronica composed her features and rode stone-faced into the ring. She took her ribbon and joined the line of riders. Lisa saw her look searchingly around the ring and was sure that Veronica was wondering who among the remaining riders could possibly have beaten her.

There was a long, tense silence. Then Max announced with a flourish, "And finally, the Champions of the First Annual Max Regnery Junior Handy Hunter Trail Competition, a combination that showed true high-class horsemanship and teamwork throughout every aspect of today's event, Miss Emily Williams and P.C.!"

The riders burst into applause. Most of Horse Wise remembered Emily from her visit the week before, and many of them had also seen her special dismount with P.C. They cheered her as if they fully understood how much she deserved the victory.

As Emily trotted regally into the ring, Lisa kept her eyes on Veronica. She saw Veronica look at Emily and give a start of recognition. It was clear to Lisa that, until the moment Emily was handed the blue ribbon, Veronica hadn't recognized her as the girl she'd insulted the week before. Veronica had seen Emily as a disabled person, not as a rider. Now she was having to readjust her opinions, fast. She and superstar Danny had been beaten by the scruffiest—and smartest, most willing, most obedient, and *best*—horse in the class.

125

Lisa felt she'd never had a sweeter victory, even though it wasn't exactly her own. The rest of The Saddle Club seemed to agree. As Emily led the riders from the ring, Stevie stood in her stirrups and called out, "P.C. stands for Perfect Champion!"

Emily looked back, laughing. Carole and Stevie cheered. Emily pulled P.C. up to Lisa and leaned forward. "Today," she said, "*I* buy the ice cream!"

"HI, EMILY!" CAROLE greeted her as she walked through Free Rein's stable door. It was Monday afternoon, two days after Emily's triumph in the handy hunter competition.

Emily straightened from brushing P.C.'s leg. "Hi!" she said. "I wondered if you guys were coming today."

"Of course we were," Carole said. Stevie and Lisa trailed in after her and greeted Emily. "We want to keep helping here," Carole continued. "Not just because we'll get to see you, but because we really like it here."

"Ms. Payne said that a few of the volunteers want to switch away from Monday nights," Lisa added. "She says if we come a few more times, we'll be ready to start working

127

as side-walkers or leaders, and we can take their places. She said I can keep working with Toby."

"With me?" Toby came trotting into the stable.

"With you," Lisa said, smiling. She gave him a quick hug and went with him into the tack room to collect a grooming bucket for his horse.

When she and Toby came out, Stevie was entertaining the other riders, Joshua and Claire, and all the volunteers with an account of Emily's handy hunter ride. Even Joshua appeared to be paying some attention to Stevie.

". . . and after the gate," Stevie was saying, "came the creek crossing, this dangerous, rushing stream. Did P.C. hesitate? Was he afraid? No! Skillfully he plunged through the icy water, carrying Emily safely to the other side."

"Which is more than we can say for your horse," Emily cut in, smiling. "I heard Belle wanted to roll."

"What happened next, Stevie?" Claire asked.

"Next . . ." Stevie looked frantically to Carole for help.

"The V-shaped figure," Carole reminded her. She looked at Joshua standing beside her and sighed. He seemed to have faded into his own world again. He wasn't listening. Carole wondered if he knew she was there.

"Oh, right!" Stevie said, remembering. "Okay, after Emily and P.C. made it across the stream, they trotted along the trail until they came to a clearing, and right in the

128

center was this big zigzag shape made out of ground poles—"

"Big, fierce, horse-eating ground poles," Lisa supplied. "Ready to leap up from the ground and devour P.C.! But did he hesitate? Was he afraid?"

"No!" Claire and some of the volunteers answered, and the group collapsed into laughter.

"This is *my* story," Stevie told her friend.

"No, it isn't," Lisa answered. "In the first place, I was there and you weren't. In the second place, it's Emily's story."

"I guess you're right," Stevie agreed good-naturedly.

"Oh, I don't know," Emily said, patting P.C. "I think I prefer your version, Stevie. P.C. as a dragon slayer, a kind of Pony Cavalier. Anyway, I owe it all to the three of you. I couldn't have done any of it without The Saddle Club."

"Yes, you could have," Carole said. "I know we helped, but other people could have helped you."

"You did it, though." Emily's eyes were shining.

"And you had to ride the whole trail yourself. We didn't do anything to help you there."

"P.C.," Emily said. "That was all P.C."

Carole couldn't argue. She knew how much Emily had done, but she knew she would have given Starlight the credit, too. "Maybe not *all* P.C.," she said, and left it at that.

Stevie led Claire to the door of P.C.'s stall. "Look over here," she said to the little girl. "Emily hung her ribbon right here."

Claire felt it with both hands. "Oh, it's smooth!"

"It says First Place, Pine Hollow Stables." Stevie read the gold lettering on the ribbon. "There's a picture of a horse head in the middle of the rosette at the top. Emily got a new halter, too, as a prize."

Claire turned to Emily. "It's a beautiful ribbon," she said.

To Carole's surprise, Joshua moved forward. He touched the ribbon with one long, slender hand. He looked at Carole questioningly.

The others went still. "That's Emily's horse's ribbon," Carole told him softly. "P.C. won it on Saturday for being a very good horse."

Joshua studied the ribbon carefully. He turned and looked at P.C. He took two steps forward and bent his head toward P.C.'s. "Good horse," he said clearly.

Carole felt her eyes fill with tears. She looked at Emily, who was smiling at Joshua as brightly as she had on Saturday when she had won the class.

Emily turned back to Carole, her eyes shining, too. "Another victory," she said.

ABOUT THE AUTHOR

BONNIE BRYANT is the author of many books for young readers, including novelizations of movie hits such as *Teenage
Mutant Ninja Turtles* and *Honey, I Blew Up the Kid,* written
under her married name, B. B. Hiller.

Ms. Bryant began writing The Saddle Club in 1986. Although she had done some riding before that, she intensi-
fied her studies then and found herself learning right along
with her characters Stevie, Carole, and Lisa. She claims
that they are all much better riders than she is.

Ms. Bryant was born and raised in New York City. She
still lives there, in Greenwich Village, with her two sons.

Don't miss Bonnie Bryant's next exciting
Saddle Club adventure . . .

HORSE-SITTERS
The Saddle Club #53

Lisa is dying for a pair of chaps. Stevie has her eye
on a new bridle. Carole wants the latest set of videos
on riding techniques. Too bad The Saddle Club is
broke.

Then Stevie gets a brilliant idea. They'll earn
money by taking care of other people's horses. How
hard could that be? Not hard at all, they soon realize,
if they don't count a few disasters . . . like *losing* a
horse!

Saddle Up For Fun!

Join The Saddle Club

As an official Saddle Club member you'll get:

- *Saddle Club newsletter*
- *Saddle Club membership card*
- *Saddle Club bookmark*
- *and exciting updates on everything that's happening with your favorite series.*

Bantam Doubleday Dell Books for Young Readers
Saddle Club Membership Box BK
1540 Broadway
New York, NY 10036

SKYLARK

Bantam Doubleday Dell
Books for Young Readers

Name _____

Address _____

City _____ **State** _____ **Zip** _____

Date of birth _____

BFYR - 8/93